IN THE GREEK TYCOON'S BED

They're dangerously handsome and
impossibly wealthy....

They're used to having it all....

The secluded beaches of their private
islands make the perfect setting for red-hot
seduction....

These Greek billionaires will stop at nothing
to bed their chosen mistresses—
women who find themselves powerless
to resist being pleasured....

IN THE GREEK TYCOON'S BED

*At the mercy of a ruthless
Mediterranean billionaire...*

Some people know practically from birth that they're going to be writers. **CATHERINE SPENCER** wasn't one of them. Her first idea was to be a nun, which was clearly never going to work! A series of other choices followed. She considered becoming a veterinarian (but lacked the emotional stamina to deal with sick and injured animals), a hairdresser (until she overheated a curling iron and singed about five inches of hair off the top of her best friend's head the day before her first date) or a nurse (but that meant emptying bedpans. Eee-yew!). As a last resort, she became a high school English teacher, and loved it.

Eventually, she married, had four children and always, always, a dog or two or three. How can a house become a home without a dog? she asks. How does an inexperienced mother cope with babies if she doesn't have a German-shepherd nanny?

In time, the children grew up and moved out on their own—as children are wont to do, regardless of their mother's pleading that they will remain babies who don't mind being kissed in public! She returned to teaching, but a middle-aged restlessness overtook her and she looked for a change of career.

What's an English teacher's area of expertise? Well, novels, among other things, and moody, brooding, unforgettable heroes: Heathcliff, Edward Fairfax Rochester, Romeo, Rhett Butler. Then there's that picky business of knowing how to punctuate and spell, what the rules of sentence structure are and how to break them for dramatic effect. They all pointed her in the same direction: breaking the rules every chance she got, and creating her own moody, brooding, unforgettable heroes. And where do they belong? In Harlequin Presents novels, of course, which is where she happily resides now.

THE GIANNAKIS BRIDE

CATHERINE SPENCER

~ IN THE GREEK TYCOON'S BED ~

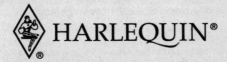

TORONTO • NEW YORK • LONDON
AMSTERDAM • PARIS • SYDNEY • HAMBURG
STOCKHOLM • ATHENS • TOKYO • MILAN • MADRID
PRAGUE • WARSAW • BUDAPEST • AUCKLAND

ISBN-13: 978-0-373-82082-5
ISBN-10:   0-373-82082-8

THE GIANNAKIS BRIDE

First North American Publication 2008.

This edition published by arrangement with Harlequin Books S.A.

® and TM are trademarks of the publisher. Trademarks indicated with ® are registered in the United States Patent and Trademark Office, the Canadian Trade Marks Office and in other countries.

www.eHarlequin.com

Printed in U.S.A.

THE
GIANNAKIS BRIDE

CHAPTER ONE

ONLY 6:46 on Tuesday, with a fine May sunrise tinting the sky over Athens a pale, translucent peach. Yet for Dimitrios Giannakis, the day was already old and too grimly familiar. He hadn't needed to hear the medical team's latest bulletin when they met for their regular early-morning consultation. One look at their faces had told him all he needed to know.

Seated in his office now, Dimitrios regarded the telephone on his desk with the kind of loathing a man might show if he thought a pit viper was about to uncoil itself from the instrument and settle in his lap. This was not a call he wanted to make. Would, in fact, have done almost anything to avoid it if he'd had any choice in the matter. But the tragic fact was, he'd run out of options. Brianna Connelly was his last hope—or, more accurately, Poppy's last hope. And when it came to his daughter, Dimitrios allowed nothing, especially not his injured male pride, to come between her and what she so desperately needed.

Of course, the odds of Brianna agreeing to his request were slim to none. She'd made it clear enough, more than four years ago, where her priorities lay: in the glossy, artificial world of high fashion, which paid homage only to youth and beauty. But he had to ask. Was willing to beg, if necessary, to give his little girl a fighting chance.

The sweep second hand on his watch inched toward seven, making it almost nine the previous evening on Canada's west coast. As good a time as any to do what had to be done.

Jaw clenched, he lifted the handset from its cradle and punched in the number for Brianna's penthouse apartment, which, fortunately, was where his sources told him she was currently to be found. Time was of the essence, and by tomorrow she could be on location in some inaccessible corner of the Sahara, Iceland or the Australian Outback. Hers, after all, was a face and a body greatly in demand worldwide, and she too inexhaustibly ambitious to reject any assignment which might further her career.

The phone rang three times before her answering service picked up and asked him to leave a message. Glowering, he swiveled his chair to face the window. "It's Dimitrios Giannakis, Brianna. It's urgent that I speak to you as soon—"

"Dimitrios?" Her voice, slightly husky and disturbingly erotic, intercepted, caressing his ear like a kiss.

Steeling himself against the sensory impact, he said curtly, "Good. You *are* there."

If he hadn't known better, he might have thought her small intake of breath signaled dismay or regret, but whatever the cause she recovered quickly and replied with matching brevity, "Obviously. What can I do for you?"

For years now he'd prided himself on being his own man, able to conquer the world and bring it to heel on his terms. The idea of groveling to anyone, least of all a woman he despised, almost made him retch. But fate had zeroed in on his one weak spot, his daughter, and although he'd have gone to his grave before he asked anything for himself, as his child's advocate, he had no choice but to swallow the bitter taste in his mouth and turn to the one person in the world who might possibly be able to help her. Alienating Brianna Connelly within seconds of contacting her was hardly the route to take.

Bearing this in mind, he attempted to soften his approach. "How are you, Brianna?"

How are you, my lovely?

Happier than I ever thought it possible to be….

Slamming shut the door on memories that were particularly inappropriate at this moment and pointless at any time, he waited for her reply.

She laughed, a brittle, uncertain sound. "Considering we haven't exchanged more than ten words in years, Dimitrios, I hardly think you care one way or the other about my state of health. Nor would I have thought we shared anything in common since my sister's death. So why don't you cut to the chase and tell me what you're really after? I have an early flight tomorrow and need to get a good night's sleep."

He should have known it was still all about her. Some things never changed.

But some things did, and swinging back to his desk again, he picked up Poppy's framed photograph, taken just six months earlier, before illness had left her little face looking so pinched and wan. Grimacing with distaste, he did what he had to do. "Very well. I have a favor to ask of you, and I warn you now, it's huge."

Four years ago, Brianna had vowed never again to set foot in Greece, and except for the time she'd attended Cecily's memorial service when she'd quite literally flown in and out of Athens on the same day, she'd stood by that promise. Yet within forty-eight hours of his latest call, not only was she in the country, she was on Dimitrios Giannakis's doorstep, deposited there by his uniformed chauffeur who'd been waiting to meet her when she landed at Eleftherios Venizelos International Airport in Spata. Changing her original travel plans had been easy enough. Her suitcases had stood already packed for her much-anticipated, month-long hiatus in Bermuda, and the clothes she'd packed—casual summertime outfits for the most part—would serve her equally well in Athens.

"I'm perfectly capable of getting myself from the airport to a hotel," she'd said, when she'd relayed her arrival date and time to Dimitrios.

He, however, had vetoed any such idea. "You will be met," he informed her flatly, "and you will be accommodated in my house where you will be pampered and cared for throughout your stay. It's the very least I can do. I am, after all, deeply in your debt."

His *house?* The word didn't come close to describing the residence confronting her now, and she hadn't even seen the inside yet. Perched on a low rise of cliff above the Aegean, and surrounded by lush gardens, its soaring white stucco exterior blushing in the sunset, the place was intimidatingly grand. Palatial, even—and Brianna wasn't exactly unused to luxury. But then, what else had she expected? She knew from experience that Dimitrios wasn't a man to do things by half.

She'd have laughed at the irony of the thought if she hadn't been so tense she could hardly breathe. Although she would never admit it, the prospect of seeing him again, let alone living under his roof, terrified her. He'd shredded her heart once and it had taken the better part of four years for it to heal. She wasn't keen on having him trample all over it a second time. Yet proximity gave opportunity for just such an outcome, especially under the present emotional circumstances.

"Well, you could have said no," her longtime agent and friend, Carter Maguire, had pointed out, when Brianna explained the reason she had to cancel all assignments in the immediate future.

To Dimitrios, yes. But how did any woman turn her back on a critically ill three-year-old?

His estate lay a few miles south of Rafina. The chauffeur, a taciturn man who'd uttered not one word during the thirty-minute drive from the airport, dumped her luggage beside her, reached forward to yank on the bell pull hanging by a chain beside the front door, then without waiting to see if anyone answered, climbed back behind the wheel of the Mercedes-Benz and drove away.

Over the fading sound of the departing car, she heard footsteps approach from inside the house and braced herself. The moment of truth had arrived. If she could weather this first meeting with Dimitrios, the worst would be over.

But the man who opened the door was too short, too genial, too bald and about twenty years too old to pass for her brother-in-law. With a mile-wide smile, he ushered her across the threshold. "*Kalispera,* Despinis Connelly, *kai kherete!* Good evening and welcome! We have been expecting you and are all so happy you have arrived."

We? She cast a nervous glance around the vast, marble-floored entrance hall, expecting Dimitrios to appear momentarily, but found nothing beyond a profusion of flow-ering shrubs in jardinieres, and a floating staircase leading to the upper floors.

The man hauled her suitcases inside. "I am Alexio," he informed her cheerfully. "I and my wife, Erika, we run the household staff. She is waiting to meet you in the court-yard with a light refreshment, and later will show you to your room. Meanwhile, I will have your luggage taken care of."

"Thank you," Brianna said. "You're very kind."

"*Parakalo*." He inclined his head. "You're welcome. Dinner will be served at nine o'clock, after Dimitrios returns."

"He's not here?"

Alexio's smile dimmed. "He's at the clinic with the little one," he explained, escorting her to the far end of the hall and through open glass doors to an inner courtyard. "He stays most evenings until she falls asleep. Most likely he will be home within the hour."

More flowering plants, a wall fountain and comfortable wicker furniture graced the tiled courtyard, making it a haven of shady tranquility, but the woman waiting to greet her wasn't quite as affable as Alexio. Although polite enough, Brianna saw reserve in her eyes, felt it in the cool touch of her hand as Alexio performed the introductions.

"You will wish to sit for a few minutes and relax after your long journey," his wife said, indicating a frosted pitcher of iced tea and bowl of fruit on the table.

Although pleasant enough on the surface, her words emerged less as an invitation than a command. Brianna, though, had been granted a short reprieve, and she wasn't about to waste it. She couldn't avoid Dimitrios indefinitely, but she could seize the chance to freshen up and look her best before she had to face him again. "That's very thoughtful of you, but I've been sitting for most of the last twenty-four hours and actually would like nothing more than to relax in a hot bath."

The woman switched her gaze to Alexio and muttered something in Greek. He responded by fanning his hands, palms down, and said quietly, "Do not fuss yourself, Erika." Then, addressing Brianna, attempted to ease the unmistakable tension in the air. "My wife is worried that she has yet to unpack your suitcases and prepare the clothes you wish to wear to dinner."

"Please don't be," Brianna told her. "I'm used to traveling and can manage perfectly well on my own."

Erika didn't quite sniff in disdain, but she came close. "Dimitrios will not like it. He has instructed us to treat you as if you are royalty."

"I'll make sure he knows that you have. Now, if you'll please show me to my room…?"

"This way, then."

As Brianna might have expected, the suite she'd been assigned outshone anything the best hotel in Athens could provide. Large and airy, it had a sitting alcove at one end beyond which a deck overlooked the sea and sprawling rear gardens whose centerpiece was a huge saltwater infinity pool. The finest linens draped the bed. A mirrored dressing room connected to a bathroom completely outfitted in travertine marble. Here was a place to which she could retreat, should things become too heated and unpleasant with Dimitrios.

"If I've overlooked anything you might need, be so kind as to let me know," Erika said woodenly, preparing to leave with Alexio, who'd followed them upstairs with the suit-cases.

Brianna cast an eye over the flower arrangements set at various points about the room, the carafe of iced water and upturned crystal glass on a tray, and remembered the array of toiletries in the bathroom. "I can't imagine there is. Nothing, that is, except—"

"Yes?"

"You mention changing for dinner. Exactly how should I dress?"

"Decently," the woman replied. "In keeping with the standards of this home."

Shocked speechless by such rudeness, Brianna simply stared at her. Apparently just as taken aback, Alexio prac-tically shoved his wife out of the room and closed the door on her before turning to Brianna again. "Erika, her English is not always the best," he offered apologetically. "What she means to say is that dinner is more…civilized than breakfast or lunch. A pretty dress will do very well, but when Kyria Giannakis was alive…" He shifted uncomfort-ably from one foot to the other. "Her ideas of what was seemly and proper did not always coincide with her husband's."

"I understand perfectly," Brianna said, and she did. Cecily had never been one to abide by anyone's rules but her own. If her behavior the last time she and Brianna had spent time together was any indication, she'd probably taken delight in flouting her husband's wishes at every turn.

Small wonder then that Erika was so hostile. She probably expected Brianna to be no better than her late twin, and who could blame her? After all, they had been identical, at least in looks, to the point that some people had never learned to tell them apart.

Especially not Dimitrios.

He was waiting in what she supposed was the living room, although "grand salon" better suited the proportions and furnishings of the long, elegant space to which Alexio directed her, just over an hour later. His hair still damp from a recent shower, Dimitrios stood in profile just outside a pair of French doors standing open to the night, a glass of amber liquid cradled in his hand, and Brianna's first thought on seeing him was that she'd overdressed for the occasion.

He wore a long-sleeved white shirt but no tie, and his trousers, though beautifully tailored, were light gray, his shoes Italian leather loafers. She, on the other hand, had put on the only dinner dress she'd brought with her. Of black silk jersey, which traveled well and took up almost no room in a suitcase, it draped softly over one shoulder, left the other one bare, and fell almost to her ankles. Platinum hoops studded with tiny diamonds swung from her ears and she'd pinned up her hair in a sophisticated swirl on top of her head. That, in combination with the three-inch heels of her strappy black sandals, left her standing close to six feet tall. Even so, when he crossed the room to greet her, he loomed over her by a good three inches, and she had to tilt her head to meet his dark gaze.

She thought she was prepared. That nothing he said or did could touch her. That she could withstand anything he threw at her—his scorn, his hostility—and that they would bounce off the hard shell of her indifference and return to him a hundredfold. But seeing him again flung her headfirst back into that painful abyss of longing she'd fought so desperately to overcome.

He was still so lean and hard and sexy that her mouth ran dry at the sight of him. She'd forgotten how big he was, how his thick black hair curled a little, no matter how severely he tried to tame it. She'd forgotten how beautiful he was, and how his mouth curved in a half smile when he was amused and trying not to show it. She'd forgotten how it felt to be the woman who was the object of his attention.

"Well, Brianna, I never thought so much time would pass before we met again, nor that it would be under such trying circumstances," he said, shaking her hand.

The last time she'd seen him—apart from a fleeting encounter at Cecily's funeral—he'd held her in his arms and begged her to stay the night with him in his stateroom. He'd been naked, his aroused flesh, hot and urgent, pressed against her, even though they'd made love as recently as fifteen minutes earlier. It had taken every last ounce of willpower for her to leave him.

It took even more to feel his fingers close so impersonally around hers now, and not tremble from the contact, brief though it had been. "I hope I got here in time."

"For dinner? Yes. We won't sit down to eat for a few minutes yet."

"That's not what I meant, Dimitrios. I was referring to your little girl. How is she?"

"Poppy's condition remains unchanged." He turned to where various decanters stood on a side table alongside a silver ice bucket containing an open bottle of champagne. "May I offer you something to drink?"

"I don't know," she said. "Am I allowed alcohol?"

She hoped she was. Normally not much of a drinker—an occasional glass of wine was her limit—just then she was rattled enough to latch on to anything that might fortify her.

"Let's ask the expert," he said, and flung an inquiring glance over his shoulder. "What do you think, Doctor? May she have a little champagne?"

Footsteps, light as a dancer's, fell into the silence following his question, and a moment later the figure of a woman somewhere in her late twenties or early thirties appeared from the shadows of the moon-washed terrace beyond the French doors. "I don't see why not. A glass or two of wine isn't going to make any difference one way or the other."

"Glahss," she'd said, her well-modulated voice overlaid with a distinctly English accent.

Approaching Dimitrios, she held out her own empty crystal flute. "In fact, I wouldn't mind a refill myself, if you're offering. Might as well take advantage of a night off. It doesn't happen often enough to go uncelebrated."

Blond, petite and elegant in a pencil-slim black skirt and pale-pink blouse, she barely reached Dimitrios's shoulder. Beside her, Brianna felt like an Amazon.

Dimitrios cupped her elbow and favored her with a smile so warm, it was a wonder the woman didn't melt on the spot. "My dear lady, you may have as many refills as you please." Then, managing to tear his attention away long enough to spare Brianna a cursory glance, supplied, "This is Doctor Noelle Manning, Brianna. She's the head of the transplant team looking after my daughter. I decided it was a good idea for you to meet her as soon as possible, since she's obviously much better able than I am to answer any questions you might have. And this," he continued, swinging his gaze back to the diminutive Noelle with all due speed, "is my late wife's sister, Brianna Connelly. You might have heard of her."

He made it sound as if Brianna topped the FBI's Most Wanted list, but if Noelle Manning noticed, she chose not to comment.

"Both heard of and seen in all my favorite magazines. Hers is not a face easily forgotten." The doctor smiled and extended her delicate little hand. "I'm sure I don't have to tell you how pleased I am to meet you, or how much is riding on your decision to come here."

In the course of her career, Brianna had met more than a few dukes, princesses, reigning monarchs and celebrities. None had left her feeling as tongue-tied and awkward as this tiny, self-assured woman. "Thank you," she managed, trying not to stumble over her reply. "I hope I'll be able to help."

"We'll find out soon enough."

"When will you begin the tests?"

"We'll give you a few days to recover from your journey, then get started." She steered Brianna to a couch beside the fireplace, took a seat on the one across from it and, tilting her head, asked, "How much do you know about the procedure, Brianna?"

"About as much as I know about my niece's illness, which is next to nothing."

"Brianna has other priorities," Dimitrios remarked, pouring the champagne. "Aplastic anemia and bone marrow transplants don't fall within her range of interests."

"How would you know?" Brianna shot back, the barely concealed contempt she'd noted in his voice cutting as sharply as a knife sliding between her ribs.

He sauntered over to hand them their drinks, then dropped down on the couch next to Noelle Manning, close enough that his knee almost touched hers. "I know my daughter will turn three in another month, and this will be the first time you've met her."

"And I explained the reason for that when you phoned."

"I know only what you choose to tell me."

"I think we all understand that time has a habit of slipping away from us," Noelle interrupted smoothly. "What matters is that you're here now, Brianna, and Dimitrios is very grateful for that." She pinned him with a forthright stare. "Isn't that right, Dimitrios?"

"Yes," he admitted, looking a little shamefaced. "You're our last hope, Brianna."

"Well, not quite," Noelle amended. "There's always the chance of an anonymous donor being found, but that could take a very long time, and Poppy…"

She didn't finish. She didn't have to. Her meaning was clear enough. Time wasn't on Poppy's side.

"I'm quite willing to begin the tests tomorrow," Brianna said. "In fact, I'd prefer to. Surely the sooner we get started, the better?"

Noelle shook her head. "Donating bone marrow isn't exactly a walk in the park, Brianna, and it would be unprofessional of me, if not criminally negligent, to allow you to go ahead without first making sure you have a thorough understanding of all that's involved."

"If it's a matter of money—"

"It has nothing to do with money," Dimitrios cut in sharply. "Your expenses will be covered."

"But I can afford—"

"So can I."

He was impossible. Arrogant, intransigent and just plain unpleasant! Why she'd once thought, even for a minute, that he was a man she could love, escaped her.

Pointedly ignoring him, she met Noelle's calm gaze. "Can we discuss this at another time? Privately?"

"Of course. I was about to suggest exactly that. Tomorrow, if you're up to it, although I understand if you'd rather wait another day. Crossing ten time zones in twenty-four hours is a bit much."

"I've been doing it for years and trained myself long ago to sleep on airplanes."

"Then it's a date. Say about noon? I'll be through surgery by then."

"Noon will be fine."

"Good. You'll arrange for your driver to bring her to the clinic, won't you, Dimitrios?"

He grunted assent and stared moodily into his glass. Unperturbed, Noelle smiled and raised hers. "Cheers, then. Here's to you, Brianna, and a long and happy relationship with your niece."

About to swallow a mouthful of whatever it was he was drinking, Dimitrios almost choked on it instead.

CHAPTER TWO

HE WAS behaving like a boor, knew it and couldn't help himself. And all because she hadn't changed, and watching her, noticing again the perfect posture, the graceful movement of her body, was driving him crazy.

He'd hoped that, like Cecily, she was beginning to lose her looks. Fat chance. If anything, she was more beautiful than ever. The same long, luscious legs and narrow, elegant hands. The same flawless ivory skin and thick, shining fall of ebony hair. The same amazing ice-blue eyes, whose clear, heavily lashed glance could paralyze a man's mind and leave him drooling like an idiot.

Erika served lamb for dinner. Flavored with rosemary and roasted on a spit over an open fire to succulent tenderness, it was one of his favorites, but that night, he could hardly keep it down. Brianna, of course, ate with her customary restraint, refusing the potatoes and helping herself to only a small portion of the meat, although she made inroads on the salad. She barely touched her wine and passed on the honey-and-fig compote dessert. Only Noelle ate with any relish, packing away a surprising amount of food for such a little woman.

After the meal they returned to the living room, and

although neither guest took him up on his offer of metaxa, they both accepted coffee. "What's it like, being a world-famous model?" Noelle asked, settling herself kitty-corner from Brianna on the couch.

"Very hard work, very long hours and not nearly as glamorous as most people think."

"Sounds a bit like my life."

"Hardly," Brianna said, with exactly the right degree of charming modesty. "I wouldn't presume to compare the two. Unlike you, I don't have any special skill or expertise. I've certainly never saved a life."

"You might. And that you're willing to try puts you on a pedestal in my eyes. As for your not having any special skills, I rather doubt that's true. It must take enormous patience and stamina to meet the artistic and, I imagine, often conflicting demands of photographers and couturiers."

Brianna gave an elegant little shrug, a studied response designed to draw attention to her upper body, he was sure. Why else would she have chosen to wear a dress that left one shoulder bare? "On occasion, yes."

Clearly fascinated by a way of life so far removed from her own, Noelle tucked her legs under her and settled more snugly into the couch. "What drew you to modeling in the first place?"

"My mother got us started when my sister and I were still in diapers, and it more or less took on a life of its own from there. While other children our age played in the sandbox or learned to ride a bike, we traveled from one junior beauty pageant to another."

"She must have been very proud of you."

"She marketed us ruthlessly," Brianna said flatly.

For a second Dimitrios thought he heard an edge of bitter resentment in her reply, then decided he must have been mistaken. She might not have had any choice when she was still a minor, but as an adult, if she didn't like what she did for a living, she could have chosen something else. She wasn't completely without brains, was she?

"And did it very successfully," he remarked, trying to keep his scorn under control. "Admit it, Brianna. You and Cecily became international celebrities before you were in kindergarten."

"Because, as you very well know, Dimitrios, there were two of us and we looked identical. *That's* what made us special."

"Now there's only you, but you seem to be doing just fine on your own."

"Losing a sister is never easy," Noelle said, flicking him a cautionary glance, "but it must have been particularly difficult to lose a twin. You were very close, I'm sure."

"When we were children, yes."

That was just one lie too many for him to stomach. "Oh, come on, Brianna! You were thick as thieves when I met you."

She turned a slow stare his way. "If you believe that, it just goes to show how little you knew either one of us."

"I was married to Cecily, remember?"

"I'm hardly likely to forget."

"Of course you aren't," he jeered, knowing that by continuing to goad her, he was pushing his luck, but unable to stop. "After all, look how you aided and abetted her in getting me to the altar."

Her mouth dropped open in shock, the delectable curve

of her lower lip stirring memories of a time when he'd explored it at erotic leisure. But he wasn't fooled. He knew better than most how she and her twin had impersonated one another when it suited their purpose.

Recovering, she said, "I dropped everything to come here at a moment's notice because you asked me to, Dimitrios. I can leave just as quickly."

"This isn't about you, Dimitrios, it's about Poppy," Noelle reminded him, electing herself mediator of a situation fast deteriorating past a point of no return. "Let's not forget that."

"Of course not." He ventured to meet his sister-in-law's icy-blue stare. "Forgive me, Brianna. I'm worried sick about Poppy, but that hardly justifies my belaboring you with it."

"I understand." Again, she tilted one shoulder in that tempting little shrug. "I'd have come sooner, if I'd known."

"You're here now, and that's what matters." Noelle set her cup and saucer on the coffee table and unfolded her legs from beneath her. "And, pleasant though it is sitting here and being spoiled, I'd better be off and catch up on my sleep. I enjoyed meeting you, Brianna."

Smiling, Brianna rose in one fluid movement. "I enjoyed it, too."

"I'll see you tomorrow, at noon?"

"I'm looking forward to it."

"Excellent! Walk me out, Dimitrios?"

"Sure."

Noelle waited until they reached her car and were well out of earshot of anyone in the house, before rounding on him. "Tell me, Dimitrios Giannakis, just how badly do you want your daughter to get well again?"

"More than anything in the world, as you very well know."

"Then I suggest you keep your tongue and your temper on a very short leash. Your behavior tonight was inexcusable."

"You might not think so, if you knew the history between Brianna and me."

"I don't give a rat's behind about your history! The only person I care about is Poppy, and I will not sit idly by and watch you systematically sabotage what might turn out to be her best chance of recovery."

"Brianna isn't all she seems."

"Really? I consider myself a pretty good judge of character and she struck me as a very nice, sincere woman."

"You didn't see past the beautiful face."

"I'm not the one hung up on her looks, Dimitrios. You are. And I strongly recommend you get over it."

"Easier said than done," he grumbled, helping her into her car. "She's a carbon copy of her sister."

Noelle laughed. "Identical twins usually are, dear!" she said and, engaging the gears, roared off into the night.

No sooner had they disappeared outside than Brianna escaped upstairs to her room. She and Dimitrios were like oil and water, never meant to mix. If Noelle Manning hadn't been there to referee, they'd have been at each other's throats by now. But they had to find a way to get along, and she could only hope a good night's rest would leave them both more kindly disposed toward each other by morning.

Erika or one of her minions had turned down the bed, switched on a reading lamp and left two English-language magazines on the nightstand. The French windows in the sitting area stood open, their filmy white drapes pulled back and hanging still as mist at each side. Over the arm of the love seat lay a shawl of softest mohair. A sterling silver tray holding an exquisite bone china hot chocolate pot and mug waited on the coffee table. Regardless of whether or not she approved, Erika was obeying to the letter her instructions to treat the guest like royalty.

But then, from what Brianna had seen, *palatial* was the key word at the villa Giannakis. She'd barely been able to concentrate on the evening meal, she'd been so bowled over by the magnificence of the setting. His dining room must have been fifteen by thirty feet, with a marble-tiled floor and priceless Savonnerie rug. Original artwork worth a king's ransom hung on the walls.

The table, large enough to seat twenty with ease, consisted of a square slab of beveled glass supported by pillars fashioned after Doric columns. Five chairs upholstered in rich cranberry fabric lined each side. A fabulous old carved sideboard and sleek sterling candelabra completed the decor, resulting in a marriage of antique and modern; of classic elegance and good taste.

A sharp departure from her penthouse which, although overlooking the strait separating the mainland from Vancouver Island, and furnished with its own kind of elegance, didn't compare to this place, which oozed comfort and opulence at every turn. And yet she'd have given anything to be back there now, mistress of her own fate.

But that wasn't an option. She was here in Dimitrios's home, if not exactly a prisoner, then certainly not a cherished guest, either.

Too keyed up to sleep, Brianna kicked off her shoes,

tucked the shawl around her shoulders and stepped out on her deck. Moonlight spilled over the sea and dappled the garden with shadows. Apart from the soft sigh of waves on the beach below, the night was utterly quiet, utterly peaceful—until a rap at the door shattered it, that was.

"Brianna," Dimitrios announced, too loudly for her to pretend she hadn't heard him, "it is I."

How painfully formal and grammatically correct, she thought wryly, refusing to acknowledge the frisson of apprehension his voice inspired. "If you've come to continue needling me," she began, opening the door, "you can take yourself and your—"

"I have come to apologize. Again. And to ask if we can forget the past, not just for Poppy's sake, but for yours and mine. This business of donating bone marrow amounts to more than a few minutes in a doctor's office. The tests are exhaustive, and I have no wish to make your time here any more unpleasant than it has to be."

"Well, if tonight's any example…"

"It's not. I'm afraid I'm never at my best after I come back from the hospital, but that scarcely excuses my taking out my anxiety on others, especially not you." He offered his hand. "May we please start over?"

She could cope with his hostility, his bad behavior. Let him snipe and rant until the earth stopped turning, if he chose. He couldn't hurt her that way, not anymore. But in his present conciliatory mode, he was downright dangerous. Enough that the resentment she'd harbored all these years suddenly seemed not so well-founded, after all, and how stupid a conclusion was that when all the evidence pointed to the contrary? "I'm not sure it's possible," she said, struggling to shore up her sagging defenses.

Taking her by surprise, he slid his fingers around her wrist in a warm, close grip. "Can we at least talk about it, and try to find a way?"

She wrenched her arm free and stepped back, horrified by the way her pulse leaped at his touch.

She'd have done better to stand her ground because he took her retreat as an invitation to march right into the room and close the door. It was all she could do not to run for cover behind the love seat. Trying not to hyperventilate, she clutched the cashmere shawl tightly at her throat.

The suite was generously proportioned. Even allowing for what the furniture occupied, there was still almost enough floor area left for a Las Vegas chorus girl to put on a show. Yet he seemed to swallow up the space until it shrank to the size of a shoe box. "What's the matter, Brianna?" he inquired silkily, closing in on her. "Are you afraid I might kiss you—or just afraid you might like it too much to try to stop me?"

"Neither," she replied, and suppressing a tug of something suspiciously like desire, she drew herself up to her full five foot nine in an attempt to stare him down.

She might as well have spared herself the effort. "Really?" he purred. "Why don't we find out?"

His arm snaked around her waist and pulled her close. The feel of his body against hers sent the blood thrumming through her veins. The lightning rod that was his mouth brought back in vivid recall the memory of the first time he'd kissed her, and where it had led: to a rendezvous in his stateroom, and an introduction to the pleasures of lovemaking, of sex, that had spoiled her for any other man.

But she remembered, too, what came afterward. The betrayal, the abandonment, had almost killed her. Although she'd honored her modeling assignments, smiling through her pain, covering up the dark circles under her eyes, everyone had noticed something was wrong. Rumors that she was ill—anorexic, bulimic, on the verge of a breakdown—had circulated like wildfire and almost destroyed her career.

You've got to show them you're still on top, Carter had urged. And she had. Because her career was all she had left. Dimitrios had robbed her of everything else.

She couldn't let him do it again.

Lifting her hands, she pushed against the solid wall of his chest with all her might. "That might be your idea of starting over, but it's certainly not mine."

He released her willingly enough. "Forgive me for allowing my baser instincts to get the better of me," he said, aloof disdain written all over his cold, beautiful face. "Believe me, I know better than anybody that what happened between us in the past is long ago over and done with, and nothing either of us can say or do will ever change that."

"At least we're agreed on one thing."

"More than one, I hope. I'm calling for a truce, Brianna, because the future—Poppy's future—is all that matters now." He wiped a hand down his face, and all at once weariness softened the severe cast of his mouth and left him looking achingly vulnerable. "They tell me what's happened to her isn't my fault, but I blame myself anyway. If I'd been a better father, paid closer attention to her, she might not be in such bad shape now."

Touched despite herself, Brianna said, "I'm sure you were, and are, an exemplary father, Dimitrios."

"No." Restlessly, he paced to the French doors and stared out. "I ignored her symptoms. She had what appeared to be a cough and a cold, and I did nothing about it for the better part of two months. It wasn't until I noticed she had bruises that couldn't be accounted for that I insisted on a more thorough investigation into the possible causes."

"Surely you'd consulted a doctor before that?"

The question was out before she could contain it, and he swung around, his face a mask of hurt and anger. "Of course I did! Within a week of her cold first appearing. I'm not a complete imbecile."

"Then if indeed there's blame to be assigned, surely it lies with her doctor?"

Again the fire went out of him. "It lies with me," he muttered, dropping down on the love seat. "It's a parent's job to protect his child. He should instinctively sense when something's not right, and maybe I would have, if I hadn't been away half the time, looking after business."

"But, Dimitrios," she said, "that's what fathers do. They go out and make a living so that their children have a decent roof over their heads, food on the table and clothes on their backs."

"There's a big difference between working to live, and living to work."

"I'm not sure I understand."

He cast her an oddly cynical glance. "Ambition can consume a person—and you ought to know."

"What's that supposed to mean?"

A muscle twitched in his jaw. "Nothing," he said, averting his gaze. "Just that, in your line of work, you have to…stay on top of your game."

"Well, yes. But don't you think that's true of anyone who wants to succeed, regardless of what they do?"

"Not if winning becomes more important than anything else. Because somebody always ends up paying. In my case it happened to be my daughter."

"You give yourself too much credit, Dimitrios. You aren't responsible for Poppy's illness. It happened despite you, not because of you. None of us ever has total control of the world around us. Sometimes fate plays a dirty trick and all we can do is find a way to live with it."

He pinned her in a mesmerizing stare. "Are you speaking from personal experience?"

Not five minutes earlier he'd said that the past was over and done with and the future was all that counted. But the way he was looking at her now was *all* about the past. It hung between them, as vibrantly alive as if it had happened just yesterday. The memories tore at her, making her ache for what might have been. And for the man she'd thought he was.

"Brianna?"

He felt it, too. It was there in the sudden deepening of his voice when he spoke her name. It swirled in the air between them—an awareness so acute she felt herself melting in its heat.

"Yes," she said, hating that she sounded so breathless. "I learned to move on when dreams I held dear didn't materialize."

"Any regrets? Ever wish you'd held on to those dreams, instead of letting them go?"

Cecily's triumphant voice echoed down the years. *Face it, Brianna, it's over. He tried both of us and chose me. We were married, just last week. Sorry there wasn't time to send you an invitation....*

Hardening her heart, Brianna said, "No. Do you?"

"Hell, yes," he said grimly. "I wish I could have given

Poppy a mother who cared. But there are some things money can't buy."

"Are you always so uncomplimentary about my sister?"

He flung another forthright gaze her way. "What do you want me to say, Brianna? That she was the best wife a man could wish for? Well, sorry to disappoint you, but there's a limit to how far I'm willing to go to preserve your illusions. The plain fact is, marrying Cecily was the second-biggest mistake of my life."

"What was the first?"

"You were," he said, surging to his feet and towering over her. "You and that damnable cruise to Crete. I should never—" He blew out an exasperated breath and raked his hand through his hair.

"Well, don't stop now. You never should have what?"

"Never mind! I've already said too much." He strode to the door and yanked it open. "Thank you again for coming. Get some rest. You're going to need it."

And having stirred up memories of the most painful period of her life, he left her.

So much for leaving the past in the past....

They'd stopped in Athens en route to London and Vancouver; a two-day rest between flights only. At least, that was the original plan, until the invitation was hand-delivered to their suite at the Grande Bretagne, the evening before they were scheduled to leave.

In marked contrast to Brianna's uninterested reaction, Cecily had almost fallen over herself with glee. "It sounds divine! I want us to accept, I really do! If you won't go for yourself, do it for me." She'd pinned on her most beguiling smile. "*Please,* Brianna? *Pretty* please?"

"Honestly, Cecily, I'd rather not. This is the first break we've had in months, and I'm ready for a rest. But there's no reason you can't go, if you're all that keen. We're not joined at the hip."

"You know full well having both of us there is the coup they're after. One of us doesn't have the same cachet."

"For heaven's sake, we're professional models, not a circus act."

"And all you ever think about is work." Cecily's tone crossed the line from wheedling to whining. "If you're so damned eager to take a rest, why can't you do it floating around the Mediterranean on a luxury yacht? What's so hard to take about that?"

"We don't know anyone else, for a start. These people so anxious to have us on board aren't friends, Cecily, they're collectors whose idea of scintillating dinner conversation is dropping the names of the celebrities they've rubbed shoulders with."

"And we're highly collectible!"

Brianna sighed. They'd argued this point more times than she cared to count, and were never going to agree. "We're a couple of reasonably pretty women who look so much alike, most people can't tell us apart. They might recognize our faces, but they haven't a clue who or what we're really about, and nor do they care. We're nothing more than novelties."

"Maybe it'll be different this time. Maybe these hosts enjoy meeting new people and showing them a good time."

Tired of riding the same pointless merry-go-round yet again, Brianna had welcomed the arrival of their manager, Carter Maguire, who occupied the suite next door. As usual after a successful assignment—and this last had been a triumph both on the runway and at the photography shoots—he'd brought a bottle of champagne. Her relief, though, was short-lived when he told them that he, too, was to join the yachting party. Was, in fact, largely responsible for the three of them having been invited in the first place.

"Too bad you wasted your time," Cecily informed him petulantly, when she heard. "Brianna's refusing to go. Thinks I should put in a solo appearance."

"Out of the question." Calmly he uncorked the champagne and filled three flutes, handed one to Cecily and shooed her out to the balcony. "Go enjoy the view, and leave me to talk to her." When she was well out of earshot, he faced Brianna. "This isn't so much an invitation as a command performance, sweet pea. These people are big names in the fashion industry and we need the contacts. You've been at the top for a long time now, but we're in danger of losing that spot, and I think we both know why." He cast a quick glance over his shoulder. "Cecily's screwed up a few times too many, and word's getting around that she's not reliable. That business in Bali last month made big headlines."

The reminder of her sister's drunken display at a night club made Brianna blush all over again. "I know. People don't forget that kind of thing in a hurry."

"Especially not in this business. And not to put too fine a point on it, but time isn't exactly on your side anymore. You'll be twenty-four in August. The next couple of years are critical—for all of us." He'd given her the lopsided grin she knew and loved so well. "Come to that, I'm no spring chicken myself. The way I see it, when you decide to call it quits, I will, too."

"That's ridiculous, Carter! You're only fifty-three, and

there are hundreds of models who'd give their right arms to have you represent them."

"Not interested." He shook his head. "When I've worked with the best, why settle for the rest? There'll never be anyone like the two of you, Brianna—or at least, there never used to be. Now…" He shrugged and raised his eyebrows in a way that spoke more eloquently than words.

Cecily wandered back into the room at that point and helped herself to more champagne. "Straightened her out yet, Carter?"

"I'm not sure." He turned a smiling glance on Brianna, but the message in his eyes was sobering. "Have I?"

She knew how much she and Cecily owed him. Until he came into their lives, they'd been pawns; children at the mercy of a mother who'd exploited them for their appearance, without any regard for their moral or intellectual well-being. She'd looked at her daughters and seen only dollar signs. The money they brought in, she spent. On herself.

Brianna and Cecily had grown up on a litany of familiar refrains.

I don't care if your feet hurt in those shoes….

Forget about joining the library. Reading books isn't going to pay the rent….

And always, as regularly as one season followed another: *You owe me…. I could've gotten rid of you and had some sort of life for myself, but I didn't. I carried you to term…raised you all by myself because your dumb-ass father fell off a ladder and broke his neck before you were even born, and left not a red cent of insurance to provide for his brats….*

The ultimate irony, of course, was that "the brats" had inherited their father's looks, as was evident from the one photograph, taken on his wedding day, which their mother had for some reason chosen not to throw away.

Fortunately, when the awkward teenage years had arrived and "the brats" weren't quite as saleable, she'd handed over the job of marketing them to an agency, and Carter had come into their lives. It had taken him less than an hour to ascertain their mother's measure and half that time to draw up a contract giving him sole control of their professional future.

Through his intervention, they'd received a decent education. He hired a lawyer and a financial consultant to protect and invest their earnings against the day when they might not be in demand as models any longer, or decided they'd rather pursue a different career. He became the family they'd never known, the one person in the whole world they could always rely on.

And now, for the first time, he was asking for something in return. How could she refuse him, especially for so small a favor?

"Yes, you've convinced me," she said. "Lazing around on board a luxury yacht for two or three weeks isn't such a bad idea, after all."

Nor was it, until Dimitrios Giannakis taught her the folly of trusting a stranger, and broke her heart in the process....

She hated the kind of people functions such as the one on the yacht attracted: women in desperate search of a rich husband, and if he happened to be ninety and so frail he could drop dead at any minute, so much the better; men who drank too much and felt their wealth and importance entitled them to paw any women who caught their fancy. She'd fended off dozens in her time, revolted by their excesses, enraged by their arrogance and condescension. She was not impressed by their studiously acquired tans, their expensively capped teeth, their hair implants. She had nothing but contempt for their boastful swaggering. Did they think what showed on the surface defined who they really were? Did they ever look at her and see past the glamorous veneer to the person underneath—one with a working brain and a heart that felt hurt and embarrassment just as keenly as anyone else?

But Dimitrios Giannakis was different. Slightly aloof and rather amused by the jostling for attention, the artificial laughter, the superficial conversation, he appeared content to socialize mostly within his own exclusive circle of friends and acquaintances. Yet when called upon to mingle, he did so with grace and charm. An acknowledged billionaire in his own right, he was rumored to be enigmatic, reserved, powerful and, when occasion called for it, utterly ruthless.

Not a man to lock horns with, from all accounts, but definitely one to admire from a distance for his cosmopolitan sophistication, his wit and, yes, his extraordinary male beauty to which even she, accustomed as she was to the most handsome of the species, was not immune.

He stood a good head taller than anyone else on board. Had a cleft in his chin, eyelashes an inch long and a mouth designed to stir a woman to outrageous fantasies. By mid-afternoon, his square, clean-cut jaw was dusted with a five-o'clock shadow. His high, patrician cheekbones were surely the legacy of some royal ancestor.

Below the neck he was no less impressive. His body, whether clad in an elegant dinner jacket or swimming trunks that defied gravity and clung to his lean hips by sheer willpower was, in a word, perfection. Strong, lean, sleekly muscled and, like his rare smile, dauntingly sexy, it epitomized masculine virility at its most potent.

She caught his attention when she sat across from him at dinner on the verandah deck, on the fifth night. Between courses, a few couples danced under the stars. Cecily sat at another table, engrossed in the leader of a rock band who was busy plying her with flattery and probably too much alcohol, but Carter was keeping an eye on her.

Not in the least interested in the latest celebrity gossip among those remaining at her own table, Brianna had smothered a yawn and glanced up to find Dimitrios's amused gaze fixed on her face.

"Do I take it," he murmured, his English so fluent only a trace of accent betrayed his Greek heritage, "that you find the conversation less than enthralling?"

"Oh, dear!" she said ruefully. "Does it show?"

"I'm afraid so." He rose and extended his hand. "Allow me to come to the rescue."

She'd have liked to say she wasn't in such dire straits that she couldn't rescue herself, but hypnotized by his faint smile and the hint of dark mystery in his eyes, she responded without a moment's hesitation. Docile as a lamb, she placed her hand in his.

Love at first sight? Until she met Dimitrios Giannakis, she hadn't believed in it. Fifteen minutes in his arms, with her body pressed close to his and his breath ruffling her hair, and she decided differently.

And paid a terrible price for doing so.

CHAPTER THREE

THE private clinic where she was to meet with Noelle Manning was in Kifissia, a northern suburb of Athens, just over half an hour's drive west of Rafina. The road wound over Mount Penteli, a fairly sparsely populated area of pine-scented forests, with the occasional very grand house interspersed among acreages whose little old cottages were as much a part of the landscape as the grape vines and olive trees planted on the land. Traffic was light, consisting mostly of agricultural vehicles, although once the Mercedes passed a truck carrying massive slabs of marble.

Set in spacious grounds on a quiet crescent high above the city, the clinic rose sleek and white against a backdrop of leafy green trees and brilliant blue sky. A receptionist in the lobby took her name and spoke briefly into an intercom. Within minutes Brianna was escorted to Noelle's consulting room on the second floor, where the doctor wasted no time getting down to business.

For the next hour she outlined the various stages of testing a potential donor to determine if she fulfilled all the requirements for a traditional bone marrow harvest, explaining each step with the succinct clarity of a true expert in her field.

"Naturally, we've combed the international registry of unrelated donors hoping to find a perfect tissue match, but so far we've unfortunately come up empty-handed," she concluded. "And since time is very much of the essence in Poppy's case, we're faced with settling for what we call an alternative donor such as a parent, who offers a half match. Poppy's mother is deceased—"

"Yes, but what about Dimitrios?"

"He's been tested, but is unable to help his daughter." Noelle lowered her glance to the open folder on her desk and closed it with gentle finality. "Obviously, I can't discuss the details with you. Professional confidentiality and all that, you understand."

"Of course."

"We're very lucky that Poppy's mother happened to have an identical twin. If it turns out that you're a suitable donor and you're willing to go through with this procedure, Brianna, you really will be giving your niece the gift of life."

"I'm absolutely willing. Nothing you've told me today has changed my mind about that."

"Do you have any questions?"

"Yes. What comes next?"

"I'll book you for a complete physical assessment—and I do mean 'complete'. By the time that's over, there'll be nothing about your health, past or present, that we won't know. We do this for two reasons. One is to make sure you're a suitable donor, free of infectious diseases—this being a fairly significant factor in your case, given the amount of foreign travel your work involves—and the other is to protect you. We gain nothing by saving one life if, in doing so, we compromise another. Once we've cleared those hurdles, we'll begin the actual protocol as I've explained it to you."

"All right, then. When can we get started?"

Noelle smiled. "I love your enthusiasm and certainly don't want to say or do anything to diminish it, but this whole undertaking has been sprung on you out of the blue, and I must therefore insist you take some time to absorb just what it involves."

"How much time?"

"A few days. A week maybe."

"But why? You've told me everything I need to know."

"No. I've told you what to expect in terms of the surgical procedure as it affects you, should you prove to be a suitable donor."

"Why do I get the feeling the other shoe's about to drop?"

"Because that's the easy part. It's what comes, or might come next, that's not so predictable." She rested her forearms on her desk and fixed Brianna in a candid gaze. "Sometimes a transplant just doesn't work. Should this happen with Poppy, it's imperative that you understand it's not your fault. Assuming you pass all the tests with flying colors, I'll be booking you for a couple of sessions with our staff psychologist, just to be sure you're prepared in the event of a negative outcome. Also, once you're approved as a donor, I'll ask you to sign a consent form. It's not legally binding and you're free to back out at any time—"

"I won't back out, Noelle. I'm committed to doing this for that poor child." Brianna leaned forward urgently. "Give me the form and I'll sign it now."

"Hear me out, please," the doctor said, holding up her

hand as if she was directing traffic. "There's more. Once you've signed that document, we'll start Poppy on a round of conditioning chemotherapy."

Brianna sank back in her chair, the information so unexpected and shocking that she felt sick to her stomach. She had a modeling friend, a stunningly beautiful young woman, who at only twenty-three had been diagnosed with leukemia. Although she was now in remission, she'd said more than once that the cure was worse than the disease.

"For heaven's sake, *why?*" Brianna cried, tears stinging her eyes. "Poppy's just a little girl—not much more than a baby—and she doesn't have cancer. Why do you have to do something so horribly drastic?"

"To destroy her abnormal cells and make room for your healthy replacement."

A logical procedure from a medical point of view, Brianna supposed. Still… "How long will it take—the treatment, I mean?"

"About a week, although the aftereffects last significantly longer, but you may be sure we'll do our best to keep her as comfortable as possible throughout that time."

"Does Dimitrios know about this?"

"Of course. I consult with him every day."

"It must be killing him!" *And I'm not making it any easier, doing battle with him over every perceived slight.*

"He's had a hard time coming to terms with it, certainly, but given the alternative, he's presented with little choice. However, the reason I'm bringing this up with you now, Brianna, is that the conditioning therapy also kills off the patient's immune system. It's therefore critical for you to understand that *if* you were to change your mind after this point, Poppy will almost certainly die or suffer serious delays in further treatment." She pushed a thick folder across her desk. "And that's why I won't let you sign anything today. I want you to go away, read this information package and weigh what I've told you before you make any final decisions."

"Poppy doesn't have time for that."

"We're talking about two weeks at the most, and Poppy is relatively stable right now."

"So stable she's in a hospital, instead of at home!"

"To protect her from exposure to infection. Even something as simple as a cold could set her back and prevent a successful transplant. Obviously, that's not a risk any of us is prepared to take."

"No, of course not." She hesitated a moment before continuing, "I'm not sure how much you know of my relationship with my sister, but you've probably gathered from remarks made at dinner last night that I've never actually met Poppy, and I'd very much like to put a face to this child who's depending on me for so much. Is it at all possible for me to visit her?"

"I don't see why not, as long as Dimitrios has no objection." Noelle glanced at the clock on her desk. "He usually stops by over the lunch hour, so is probably with her now. Why don't we go and find out?"

Brianna thought she knew all about heartache and heartbreak, but the next twenty minutes or so taught her she hadn't begun to plumb the depths of either. Not only was Poppy hospitalized, she was in isolation—what Noelle chillingly referred to as "a sterile environment"—which meant not only that she had no other children nearby to keep her company, but also that everyone going into her room first had to follow a strict hygiene regimen.

"Doesn't it frighten her, being surrounded by people whose faces she can't really see?" Brianna asked, donning the required gown and mask.

"You tell me," Noelle responded, approaching an observation window set in the wall connecting the nursery with the outer room. "Does that look like a frightened child to you?"

Following, Brianna looked through the glass, and what she saw on the other side made something deep and powerful clutch at her heart. Dimitrios sprawled in a rocking chair, reading to Poppy whom he cradled in his lap as easily, as naturally, as if it had been designed for the express purpose of holding a sick child.

His broad shoulders filled the width of his chair; his long legs, elegantly clad in finely tailored black trousers, poked out from the folds of a pale-yellow gown. Above his mask, his dark brows rose in comical dismay. Wide with feigned astonishment, his gaze swung from the book and came to rest on Poppy, and even with the barrier of glass separating them, Brianna heard her laughter.

Climbing his torso, she planted her bare little feet on his thighs and reached for the brightly colored balloon bouquet floating almost to the ceiling and anchored by ribbons to the back of the chair. From her vantage point, Brianna could see only the back of the child's head, covered with thick black hair just like her own. And soon it would be gone, falling away in clumps….

Again tears threatened, but she blinked them back and managed a shaky smile when she saw that Dimitrios had glanced up and was gesturing for her and Noelle to join him.

Poppy turned at the sound of the door opening, and for a moment, Brianna froze. Even allowing for illness robbing her of so much, the child was exquisite, her delicate little face dominated by enormous eyes the exact same shade of blue as her own and Cecily's—but with an innocence to them that Cecily had lost at a very early age if, indeed, she'd ever possessed it at all.

"Kalimera," Dimitrios said. "Hi. This is a surprise."

Until that moment Brianna had deliberately thought of Poppy as his daughter, or the little girl, or the child, or even, may God forgive her, "the patient." It had been, she supposed, her way of distancing herself from a set of circumstances still more painful to contemplate than they had any right to be. But now, suddenly, the words she'd avoided using were the only ones with real meaning. Closing the distance between herself and the chair, she dropped down to be at eye level with Poppy and said, "I thought it high time I met my niece. Hello, beautiful! I'm your auntie Brianna."

Whether or not she really understood what that meant was doubtful, but after surveying Brianna for a long, quiet moment, Poppy smiled and reached out her arms to be held. Almost choking with emotion, Brianna looked to Dimitrios to gauge his reaction.

In one lithe movement, he was out of the chair. With a jerk of his chin, he invited her to take his place, and when she was comfortably seated, passed her niece to her. Brianna felt the warm little body, the painfully fragile bones, the soft skin. She felt the sweet damp draft of breath against her cheek, the trusting clutch of tiny fingers at the side of her neck.

A fresh tide of emotion rolled over her. Her entire being

filled with something so visceral, so elemental, it left her breathless. Only once before had she known such an instant connection with another human being, and, as swiftly as she had the first time around, she fell in love again. Hopelessly, helplessly. And this time, forever.

I'm finally where I belong, she thought, dazed by sudden blinding insight. *Not on a runway or on location for a glamorous shoot, but in a simple rocking chair, with a child in my arms. Modeling might have been my occupation, but motherhood is my true vocation.*

Swallowing hard, she closed her eyes and held on: to Poppy, and to the tears she didn't want her niece to see; to the hope that she could be the one to give this little soul the gift of life; and most of all, to the chance to make up for the years she had missed being an aunt to this adorable child. When, after struggling for an interminable minute or so, she could finally breathe again, she set the rocking chair in gentle motion and began to hum a lullaby, which she neither knew how nor when she'd committed to memory. And as if she'd finally come home, Poppy relaxed and let her head settle drowsily against Brianna's shoulder.

"If I didn't know better, I'd say she recognizes you," Dimitrios said, his voice as rough sounding as if his throat had been scraped raw with coarse brown sugar.

Brianna's eyes flew open in shock. "Do you think she's mistaking me for Cecily?"

His laugh emerged, harsh, abrupt and brimming with bitter irony. "*Ohi!* Not in a million years! For a start she was only eighteen months old when her mother died. Not only that, Cecily never crooned to her or held her like that, and I'm pretty sure she never rocked her to sleep. She left that kind of job to Erika or the latest nanny."

Running her hand in slow, comforting strokes up Poppy's delicate spine, Brianna whispered, "What *did* she do for her, then?"

"Dress her up like a doll or something you'd stick on the top of a Christmas tree, and parade her before visitors to impress them. Smother her with kisses and endearments if there happened to be a captive audience on hand to applaud her. *Pretend* she cared," he finished, with such unvarnished disgust that Brianna shuddered.

It all sounded so horribly familiar; so reminiscent of her and Cecily's own blighted childhood, when their mother would deliver an award-winning performance as Parent of the Year if the "right" people were there to witness it and there was the chance she could further her ambitions to make money from her daughters. The difference, of course, was that Cecily hadn't done it for money. She hadn't needed to. She'd married it, instead.

"If that's how she felt, she never should have had a baby in the first place."

"No. You'd have been a much better choice," Dimitrios said, so quietly that Brianna wasn't entirely sure she'd heard him correctly.

But the glance he turned on her, intense and full of dark remorse, made her heart leap in her breast and sent a thread of warmth stealing through her body. But *Be careful!* her head cautioned. *He seduced you with words once before and you learned to your cost that, in the end, they meant nothing. Don't fall for the same old ploy a second time.*

From her post by the door, Noelle coughed lightly, as though to remind them of her presence and, crossing the room, lowered the high rail on the side of the hospital crib and took Poppy from Brianna. "This little one's had enough excitement for now and is falling asleep," she said, very much the doctor in charge. "The more rest she gets, the better, so let's leave her to nap undisturbed."

She placed Poppy gently on the mattress and drew a soft blanket over her lower limbs. Robbed of the warmth of that sweet little body, Brianna crossed her hands over her breast in a futile attempt to stem the emptiness that filled both her arms and her heart. *She should have been our baby,* she thought, anguished. *Mine and Dimitrios's. She'd never have had to make do with Erika or a nanny if I'd been her mother.*

Noelle touched her arm kindly. "If Dimitrios doesn't mind, you can come back later, but I have to ask you to leave her for now."

"I don't mind," he said. "It'll be a change from her having to make do with me all the time."

"Is there no one else in the family who comes to see her?"

"We have no other family," he replied with grim finality.

Poppy rested on her stomach with her head turned to one side. Her lashes lay thick and dark as soot on her pale cheeks. Her thumb had found its way into her sweet little rosebud mouth. Her little bottom rose and fell gently with each breath she took.

Brianna lingered for one last look at the new love of her life. *You do* now, *sweetheart,* she telegraphed fiercely. *You have me, and together you and I are going to beat this disease, and I'm going to be there to watch you grow up strong and healthy.*

Dimitrios was so silent and so obviously preoccupied as they rode the elevator to the main floor and walked out to the clinic's sun-filled forecourt where Spiros waited in the

Mercedes, that the last thing she expected was for him to stop her as she was about to climb into the car and say, "I don't know about you, but I'm ready for something to eat. How about we stop somewhere before you head home?"

Taken aback, she said, "You're inviting me to have lunch with you?"

"Why not?"

"Well, for a start, we might have agreed to put our differences behind us, but that doesn't mean we particularly like each other much."

"Are you so convinced of that, Brianna," he asked gently, "or is it just wishful thinking on your part?"

Both his tone and his question stopped her short. For the past several years she'd clung to the belief that he was a liar and a cheat. It had made losing him a little more bearable. After all, she prided herself on having some brains, and what woman in her right mind wanted to tie herself to a man incapable of fidelity?

Since her arrival on his doorstep, though, and from a couple of rather ambiguous remarks on his part, not to mention that unpremeditated, devastating kiss, she was no longer sure of anything. Last night, when the first doubts crept in, she'd told herself her imagination was in overdrive. Today, she'd been forced to confront a reality so stark it left nothing to the imagination.

Like it or not, she and Dimitrios were allies against a fearsome, wicked enemy. Although they were both hurting, his pain ran deeper; deep enough that he was regarding her now with a dark, almost pleading urgency that tugged at her heart.

But could she trust her heart, this time around? Could she trust *him?*

Sensing her reluctance, he said, "I'm inviting you to have lunch, Brianna, not asking you to sell me your soul, and I promise not to have your food poisoned."

"It never occurred to me that you might," she said, shaking off her doubts. "And yes, I'd very much like to have lunch with you, as long as your driver doesn't mind being kept waiting."

"I pay Spiros to be where he's needed, when he's needed. He can take us to the taverna I have in mind, or we can walk, if you'd rather. It's not too far."

Finding herself in the back seat of the Mercedes with a Dimitrios who, despite the anxieties plaguing him, grew more appealing by the second, was a bit too potent a mix for her to swallow. "It's such a lovely day, why don't we walk?"

"I hoped you'd say that." After a quick word with his driver, he cupped her elbow and steered her down the curving drive to the tree-shaded street. "Sure the heat's not too much for you?" he inquired solicitously, glancing at her cheeks, which she knew were flushed.

She was burning up, but not for the reason he thought. His touch electrified her, sending a tide of warmth riding up her neck and reviving more buried memories.

Time spun backward to another hot afternoon under a blue Greek sky. Clad in a black bikini, she reclined under an awning, on the deck of the 325-foot yacht lying at anchor in a quiet bay in the Cyclades, some sixty miles south of Athens. And Dimitrios Giannakis, a man she'd met only a few days before was tracing seductive patterns over her exposed midriff and murmuring sweet nothings in her ear.

And at the end of it all, they really were "nothings," she

reminded herself, shutting out the image. He hadn't meant a word he'd said, and she'd be a fool to read too much into the present situation. He was, after all, a sophisticated man, accustomed to moving in the upper echelons of society. Impeccable manners were as much a part of him as his black hair and beguiling smile. Taking a woman's arm as she crossed the street came as naturally to him as breathing. Or lying.

They stopped at a charming little taverna several blocks from the clinic. Tucked away on a side street, it opened at the back to a large courtyard shaded by a vine-covered pergola. About a dozen tables clustered around a fountain set in the middle, but only two were occupied, the lunch hour crowd having already been and gone.

Without consulting her, he ordered two salads and a bottle of Boutari Moschofilero. "Still your favorite Greek wine, I hope?" he queried, tipping the rim of his glass to hers, after the waiter had poured.

"Yes," she admitted, unable to stem a little glow of pleasure that he'd remembered.

"And you still don't care for ouzo?"

"Definitely not."

He fixed her in another unwavering gaze. "It's nice to know some things haven't changed, Brianna."

But some things have, she told herself sternly. *Don't let him seduce you into forgetting that.*

Their waiter reappeared and set down a basket of bread still warm from the oven and a small appetizer tray of olives and grilled octopus.

Welcoming the interruption as a chance to turn the conversation into safer, less personal channels, and hoping she sounded a lot more nonchalant than she felt, she said,

"I'm not familiar with this part of Athens. It's really quite lovely."

"Yes."

"I noticed on the way here that we passed a number of rather grand villas."

"Yes."

"Some reminded me of Victorian manor houses in England."

"Yes."

"Noelle's English, isn't she?"

"Yes," he agreed, still holding her captive in his stare.

"What made her decide to work in Greece?"

"The weather's better here?"

More unhinged by the second, she snapped, "Stop making fun of me—and stop saying 'yes' all the time."

"Okay. I don't know why Noelle chooses to work here, although I expect it's because she's free to work in any country that's part of the European Union. What I do know, and what matters to me, is that she's recognized as being one of the best in her field, the clinic's as high-tech as anything you'd find anywhere else in the world, and only the best is good enough for my daughter. Any other questions?"

"No."

"Good," he said, allowing himself a small, satisfied smile. "Then let's stop pretending either of us gives a damn about the neighborhood or Noelle's reasons for practicing medicine here instead of in England, and talk about something else."

"Like what?"

"Like us," he said. "As in you and me. And let's start with you."

CHAPTER FOUR

HE ACHIEVED the result he was hoping for, surprising her
enough that she almost dropped her wineglass. Recovering
herself just in time to set it down on the table, she raised
startled eyes to his, classic deer-in-the-headlights shock
registering on her lovely face.

Good. Perhaps by keeping her on edge, he could unearth
a few fragments of truth from all the lies. It was well past
time.

Hesitantly she said, "What do you want to know?"

"Everything, but we can begin with this morning. Now
that you have a more complete picture of what you'd be
letting yourself in for, how serious are you about going
ahead with testing as Poppy's donor?"

"I haven't changed my mind, if that's what you're afraid
of. In fact, I'm more determined than ever."

"Even though, if you turn out to be a suitable match,
you'd end up with surgical scars on those elegant hips of
yours? Won't do much for your career, will it, if you can't
strut your stuff in a bikini?"

"I haven't modeled bikinis in years, but even if that
wasn't the case, I hardly equate a couple of little scars with
saving a child's life. You might not respect how I earn my

living, Dimitrios, but I'm not quite as shallow as you seem to think."

"But you *are* ambitious. We both know that. You don't let anything come between you and your career."

"That's hardly a fair comment! There's a difference between being professional and being driven to the point that everything else runs second."

She sounded so aggrieved that, if he hadn't known better, he'd have thought she actually believed the rubbish she was spouting. Steeling himself not to soften, he said, "I could argue the point, but let's not go down that road, at least not right now. Instead tell me why you're so eager and willing to help a child you previously refused to acknowledge."

"I already explained I didn't know Poppy existed until your phone call last Tuesday."

"You don't seriously expect me to believe that, do you?"

A flush accentuated those classic cheekbones. "I don't care whether you believe me or not," she said, her eyes shooting icy, pale-blue sparks. "I'm *telling* you that the last time I spoke to Cecily was right after you married her. It was also, you might recall, the last time I spoke to you, as well—until the other day. And I have no reason to lie."

"Are you saying you didn't even know your sister was pregnant?"

"That's right. Apart from the lawyer's letter telling me she'd died, I knew nothing about her life with you. You were hardly forthcoming, after all. Even at her funeral, we didn't exchange more than the barest civilities. And contrary to what other twins might experience, Cecily and I didn't share telepathic communication."

He cradled his wineglass and regarded her thoughtfully.

"In a sick sort of way, I suppose that makes sense. Cecily didn't broadcast the news that she was expecting. In fact," he finished bitterly, "she didn't deal well with pregnancy at all."

Picking up on his black tone, she said, "What do you mean?"

"She tried to terminate it at twenty weeks."

"*No!*" Again he'd caught her off guard. Her flush drained into shocked pallor. "For heaven's sake, *why?*"

"She didn't like what it was doing to the shrine that was her precious body," he spat, the acrid taste of disgust lingering in his mouth.

"Oh." She dampened her lower lip with the tip of her tongue. "What changed her mind?"

"I did," he said, reliving the scene in all its ugly detail. "Very emphatically."

You can't make me go through with it.

Yes, I can, Cecily. And I will.

How? By keeping me under lock and key for the next five months? Appointing that benighted housekeeper of yours my prison guard?

If I have to, yes.

You don't have the right. It's my body, not yours.

But it's my child.

I hate you, Dimitrios!

I'll survive—and so will that baby....

Brianna cleared her throat. "Do you think," she began tentatively, "her trying to, um, bring on a miscarriage, is in any way responsible for Poppy being so ill now?"

"I've asked myself the same question a thousand times, and I'm told by those who ought to know that the two aren't related, but..." He shook his head, the doubts still plaguing him. "I should have kept a closer eye on Cecily. Monitored where she was going, who she was seeing. Made sure she didn't drink alcohol or worse yet, dabble in recreational drugs."

Reaching across the table, Brianna put a sympathetic hand over his, and this time he was the one taken by surprise. Up to that point, he'd initiated all physical contact between them, and, fragile though her overture was, he liked it. He liked it very much. And that was something he had to guard against.

"Don't," she said. "This was not your fault, Dimitrios. Do not blame yourself for Cecily's bad behavior."

"How do you know it wasn't my bad behavior that drove her to such extremes?"

"Because I knew Cecily. Better than you did, probably. We lived together for almost twenty-four years, remember, and it doesn't surprise me one iota that losing her figure struck her as a disaster on a par with the sinking of the *Titanic*. She was always very…" She shrugged, searching for the right word.

"Vain?"

"Conscious of her image," she amended. "It's not surprising, you know. We'd both been brought up believing how we looked was all that mattered. And I'm sorry to say, Cecily believed it. Not only that, I know for a fact that if she decided she was going to party with the wrong crowd, she'd have found a way to do it, regardless of any steps you took to prevent it."

"Are you speaking from personal experience?"

She withdrew her hand and sat back in her chair, seeming to regret having revealed so much. "She was my sister and I loved her, but…" She sighed and looked off to one side. "Look, I don't mean to sound disloyal, but for your peace of mind you need to understand that she was always…willful."

"What about you?" he asked. "Are you as much alike on the inside as you were on the outside?"

"I can be stubborn," she admitted. "When I make up my mind, I tend to stick to it."

"I guess I should be glad. Because of that, Poppy might have found a donor."

She bathed him in the kind of glance that, once upon a time, before he'd disciplined himself to separate sex from sanity, would have reduced him to a mass of raging testosterone. A soft, urgent, melting glance which, even now, he found dangerously distracting. "I might have been motivated by purely humanitarian reasons at the beginning, Dimitrios, but that changed when I actually met Poppy, when I looked into her eyes and held her in my arms." Her breasts rose in a heartfelt sigh—another distraction he didn't need. "My heart is engaged in a way I never expected. I've never before formed such an instant bond with another person."

He couldn't help himself. He had to ask. "Never, Brianna?"

Some of the animation faded from her face. "Hardly ever," she hedged. "And never with a child. Until this morning, I didn't know…"

"What?" he persisted, when she lapsed into silence.

Clearly undecided about how to answer, she bit her lip, then sat straighter in her chair, very much the posture-perfect model. "How remarkable children are. I mean, look at all Poppy's going through—being away from you and the people she knows and loves, having needles stuck in her all the time, not having other children to play with. Yet she was laughing and smiling and—"

She choked up suddenly, and he saw tears shining in her eyes. "I'm sorry," she mumbled. "I don't mean to go all weepy and emotional on you."

"No need to apologize. I have my moments, too."

She swallowed hard. "How do you do it, Dimitrios? How do you manage to hold it together when you see her?"

"Because I have to. Because if there's one thing I've learned through all this, it's that children are amazingly resilient and accepting and brave, and the least I can do is follow their example."

Again she grabbed for his hand, and this time curled her fingers around his. "I want to help you, not just by testing as a donor. I want to be with you both—see it through with you. Please let me. Please don't shut me out just because we were once…close."

"'Close,' Brianna?" He freed his hand and poured more wine into his glass. "We were *lovers,* until you abruptly decided otherwise."

She reared back in outrage. "Well, what else did you expect?"

"A truthful explanation for your very sudden departure would have been nice." He paused. "And if you couldn't do it then, how about now?"

Her eyes grew wide with astonishment. "You really want me to spell it out for you, after all this time?"

"It's never too late to set the record straight, and I'm tough. I can take rejection. What I can't tolerate are lies. So explain to me, please, why you bothered pretending you wanted to build a future with me, when all along you planned to jump ship at the first opportunity? Why didn't you just come right out and tell me your precious modeling career meant more than anything I had to offer?"

"Because that wasn't the reason, you jerk! I wanted you more than I've ever wanted anything in my life, even if I do now ask myself why, but I left because there were some things I refused to share with my sister, your bed being one of them."

He gave his head a disbelieving shake, sure he'd misunderstood. "What did you just say?"

"Oh, please! Stop pretending you don't know what I'm talking about. We made love in your stateroom. You wanted me to stay the night. I wouldn't, because I didn't want to start a feeding frenzy of gossip among the crew and passengers if we were found out. So I went back to my own quarters, but I couldn't sleep. That's the kind of effect you had on me, Dimitrios. I was intoxicated by you. Floating on air."

"You had a funny way of showing it."

Ignoring his snide interruption, she continued doggedly, "I finally decided to go up on deck and watch the sunrise. And that's when I saw Cecily leaving your cabin."

"Did you?" he said. "And did you ask her what she was doing there?"

"I didn't have to. She was only too happy to tell me what marvelous stamina you had, what an incredible romp between the sheets you'd given her."

"And you believed her."

Suddenly not sounding so confident, she muttered, "Why wouldn't I?"

"Because she was lying, Brianna," he informed her dully, none of the exhilaration he should have known filling him. Instead he felt hollow, empty. So much time wasted, so many mistakes piling one on top of another, and all because of a misunderstanding that need never have occurred in the first place. "As you'd have found out soon enough if you'd had the guts to shove her back through my door and made her repeat her allegations to my face."

"You're the one lying. I *saw* her. She'd been in your room."

"Sure she had. Tried climbing into my bed, as well, pretending to be you. It was dark enough that she might even have gotten away with it, if I hadn't picked up a whiff of tobacco on her breath."

"Did you confront her?"

"No," he said sarcastically. "I jumped up and down like a crazed ape, beat my manly chest and bellowed to the whole of Crete how lucky I was to have the Connelly twins fighting over me." He stopped and drew an irate breath. "What do you take me for? Of course I confronted her!"

"Well, what did she say?"

"That you'd asked her to keep me occupied so that you could sneak off and catch a flight out of Heraklion without my knowing."

Ashen-faced, Brianna stared at him. "But why would she bother concocting such an elaborate story for me? What advantage did that give her?"

"Use your head, woman! She wanted rid of you, because she was jealous, and she knew damned well your pride would never allow you to challenge me and thus expose her deception."

Rallying, she countered, "It's easy for you to make that claim now, when it's too late for anyone to prove otherwise."

"I'm not in the habit of lying, Brianna, and if it's a confession of guilt you're after, I freely admit I slept with her the very next night after you left," he acknowledged calmly. "A big mistake on my part, certainly, and I'm not proud of it, but a man tends to react badly when he's been dumped by the woman he planned to spend the rest of his life with. Pour enough booze into him, and if there's someone else more than willing to take her place, and she happens also to be a carbon copy of the original, well…" He shrugged. "It's called the rebound factor. Maybe you've heard of it."

"It strikes me as a bit more than that. After all, you ended up marrying her a couple of months later, and not a moment too soon, judging by Poppy's age."

She looked so crushed that, just briefly, he regretted having spoken so forthrightly. But she wasn't the only one who'd paid a high price, anymore than he was the only one who'd made mistakes.

"Because she was pregnant," he said. "Look, Brianna, I could tell you I never loved her the way I loved you, that I cursed myself a thousand times over for being such a bloody fool, and it would all be true, but none of that changes the fact that you and I, not Cecily, were mostly at fault. She seized an opportunity, but we're the ones who gave it to her because we didn't trust one another enough."

"We hadn't known each other long enough to develop any trust."

"Perhaps not, but if we'd really been as deeply in love as we thought we were, I'd have fought for you anyway and hoped like hell I wouldn't live to regret it. But I didn't. I let you go."

Again she glanced aside. "I'm to blame, as well. I ran

away because it was easier than facing what I thought was the truth. I should have known better. I just never dreamed Cecily could be so...so destructive."

"Because you didn't really know her as well as you thought. Nobody did. All we ever learned was what she allowed us to see. She was like an iceberg, with seven-eighths, the most treacherous part, hidden."

"Hindsight's a wonderful thing, isn't it?" she said miserably.

His cell phone interrupted, sparing his having to comment. Just as well. He might have said something he'd live to regret. *"Me sing khorite,"* he murmured, noticing the name showing on the display screen. "Excuse me. I have to take this call."

She nodded and, rising from her chair with her trademark grace, wandered over to examine the flowers growing near the fountain. "What?" he barked into the phone, royally ticked off with himself for not being able to tear his glance away from her long, elegant legs and slender hips.

"Where the devil are you?" Pavlos, his PA, shot back. "The meeting's due to start in ten minutes."

"What meeting?"

"The one slated to make you another cool two million euros or more, provided, of course, you're still interested. The one which has the consortium from Shanghai cooling its heels in the executive lounge and wondering if you really exist or are just a figment of an overactive Greek imagination. Need I go on?"

"Skata, Pavlos," he muttered. "I forgot all about it."

"Not surprising, I guess, all things considered. You've got a lot on your mind right now."

"More than you can begin to guess," he groaned. "Keep the visitors occupied with the video presentation until I can get there, will you? I'm still in Kifissia, but I'll be there as soon as I can. Traffic's building, so I'll leave my car here and take the Metro. I should be there within forty minutes."

Seeing he'd ended the call, Brianna returned to the table. "Everything all right?"

"*Ohi.* I have to go, but you stay and enjoy the rest of your meal and the wine. I'll take care of the bill on my way out. If you're up to exploring a bit more, you might want to browse the boutiques farther down the road." He pressed his phone into her hand. "You know how to use one of these. Spiros is on speed dial. When you're ready to leave, give him a call and let him know where to pick you up."

She caught his sleeve as he went to turn away. "Just a minute—"

"I don't have a minute, Brianna," he interrupted, making no effort to curb his impatience. "I know we were in the middle of something, but it'll have to keep until another time because I need to leave. Now."

"Just tell me before you go. Is it Poppy? Has something happened? Because if it has and you're headed back to the clinic, I'm coming with you."

He'd have had to be pretty jaded not to recognize the concern in her eyes and voice. Feeling low as dirt for snapping at her without cause, he squeezed her hand and said more gently, "It's not Poppy. It's business. But thanks for caring. Look, I'll see you later, okay, and we'll pick up where we left off. Meanwhile, try to enjoy what's left of the afternoon."

She watched him walk away, six feet plus of utter competence and self-assurance. Never a wasted word or motion.

Never an awkward pause as he fumbled for just the right word. Never a clumsy move.

She, however, was a mess. She'd been on an emotional roller coaster for the better part of three hours. And the last sixty minutes had, in some ways, been the most shocking.

She'd known for a long time that Cecily envied her; that what she herself saw as an equal partnership between sisters had, in Cecily's mind, become a competition between rivals, one that recognized no boundaries between their professional and personal lives. But that she'd go to such extremes, that she'd deliberately sabotage her sister's budding love affair…?

On the other hand, was it really so surprising? Casting her mind back, Brianna recalled a number of occasions during the last few months they'd shared an apartment, when she'd been singled out for special assignments which hadn't included her sister, but she'd missed them because Cecily either "accidentally" erased voice mail messages, or conveniently "forgot" to pass them on.

"She's spiraling into self-destruction, and she'll take you down with her if you're not careful," Carter had raged, after one particularly unfortunate incident. "Do yourself a favor and get set up in your own place before she succeeds."

But Brianna hadn't believed him. Hadn't *wanted* to believe him. "We might have our differences, but at bottom, we love each other," she'd insisted. "Cecily would never deliberately hurt me."

Now, when it was too late, she knew differently. What had begun as a slow, almost imperceptible erosion of her relationship with her sister had degenerated into outright betrayal during that cruise through the Greek islands. Yet it could all have turned out so differently if only, as Dimitrios had so astutely pointed out, they'd trusted each other. Instead they'd been too dazzled with stardust to see the danger lurking on the sidelines and guard themselves against it.

And yet it had been there all along, if only she'd recognized the signs. That first night, as the yacht set sail from the mainland and headed south to the island of Crete, their hosts had thrown an extravagant cocktail party. There were thirty-six guests gathered on deck, at least twenty-five of whom, including her and Cecily, were either famous faces or famous names on both sides of the Atlantic. The remaining eleven were a blend of wealthy sophisticates and corporate power moguls.

Of the latter, the most influential by far was the cultured Dimitrios Giannakis, whose empire, one of the group she and Cecily were with confided, ran the gamut from charter airlines to oil to real estate.

"Is he married?" Cecily had inquired, almost tripping over her own feet in her eagerness to catch a closer glimpse.

"No," the man replied on a well-bred snort of laughter. "But trust me, it's not for want of offers."

Perhaps if she herself hadn't fallen so completely under his spell, Brianna might have paid closer attention to Cecily's growing displeasure at being overlooked by the man who was undoubtedly the most eligible bachelor in Europe.

Swamped with regret for what might have been, Brianna pushed aside the remains of her lunch. She and Dimitrios had started out with such dreams. Found such bliss together, albeit for too short a time. Why hadn't they gone the extra distance and believed in each other?

Instead they'd fallen victim to one of the oldest games in the book: the fury of a woman scorned. Cecily had got what she'd been after from the start, and Brianna had lost a sister in the process. She'd never seen Cecily again, except for the occasional photograph plastered on the front page of some tabloid or other on display in the supermarket: "Former supermodel Cecily Connelly, wife of Greek billionaire Dimitrios Giannakis, at a party in Cannes…hobnobbing with the jet set in Monte Carlo…skiing in the Swiss Alps."

Cecily was always dazzling the camera with her famous smile. There was never any mention of a child. And a grim-faced Dimitrios, if he was there at all, invariably remained at arm's length from all the hoop-la.

Brianna never bought the tabloid. She never read the article. She turned away, even so small a reminder of what had been stolen from her, enough to darken her day.

CHAPTER FIVE

WALLOWING in remorse for things it was much too late to change, left Brianna too unsettled to endure the rest of the afternoon under Erika's hostile surveillance. She needed to be around people who didn't regard her as a necessary evil; with strangers who'd judge her on her own merits. So she took Dimitrios's advice and explored the streets of Kifissia.

The boutiques were lovely. If she'd been in a more frivolous mood, she could have spent a small fortune on exquisite clothes. One ensemble in particular caught her eye. A voile dress printed with pale, overblown roses in shades of pink and mauve on an ivory background, it floated over the back of an antique chair set on a circular dais in the showroom window. The hem of its voluminous skirt fell in graceful folds to where a matching hat with a wide brim lay on the silver-gray carpet, next to a pair of exquisite ivory silk pumps.

Brianna's experience with the garment industry was such that she recognized fine clothes when she saw them, and this was a gem; a special-occasion dress designed by someone with a true eye for elegance and style. But she had weightier matters on her mind, and the only special occasion in her near future was a date with a team of doctors in a private clinic. So, with a last fond glance at the dream of a dress, she continued down the street and found herself outside a shop catering to babies and small children.

The door stood open and, on impulse, she stepped inside. Stuffed toys, hand-made quilts, pint-size furniture and other nursery accessories vied for space with adorable dresses, beaded socks, dainty little shoes and lace-trimmed sun hats. Delightful outfits of the kind that Poppy should have been wearing, rather than the hospital gowns that presently comprised her entire wardrobe. But she lived in such a protected environment, she couldn't cuddle a plush teddy bear or a favorite doll. If an object couldn't be wiped off with germicidal solution morning, noon and night, it didn't get past the door to her room. Even the book Dimitrios had been reading to her had laminated pages.

Until that moment Brianna had been drawn more by idle curiosity and wishful thinking than by any serious intention of shopping for her niece. With so many restrictions in place, there hadn't seemed much point. But faced with such an abundance of riches, as it were, she suddenly found herself asking, Why not? If ever a child needed and deserved a little spoiling, that child was Poppy. Surely there was something here, some inoffensive, pretty thing that could soften the barren confines of her room without compromising her health?

The shop owner approached, and after ascertaining that the woman spoke English, Brianna explained, "I'm looking for a gift for my three-year-old niece, but it can't be clothing or anything like this." Regretfully, she picked up a gorgeous velvet rabbit with long, silky ears. "She's hospitalized, you see—and in isolation."

"She is in the children's wing of the Rosegarth Clinic?"

"I'm afraid so, yes."

"Ah." The woman clicked her tongue sympathetically. "Then certainly she needs something to make her smile when you're not there, but it must be something which will not expose her to risk of infection, yes?"

"How did you know?"

"Because you're not the first to come here, my dear lady. Many families with children at the Rosegarth end up at my door, hoping to find just the right gift to cheer up their sick little ones." She indicated a row of glass-domed porcelain figures, some perched on swings, some skating on mirrored surfaces, others riding on painted carousel horses or Ferris wheels, and all mounted on sturdy metal bases. "These are very popular. They're actually battery-operated music boxes with colored lights that rotate as the figures move. They can be kept out of reach of the patient, but still be enjoyed. I also have a wide selection of pretty mobiles—butterflies, humming birds, swans and such—which also sell very well."

Given a choice, Brianna would have left with enough packages to fill the trunk of the Mercedes, but when Spiros came to collect her, she'd managed to confine herself to one bright-red Ferris wheel music box, and a mobile of irides-cent butterflies. "Although I'll probably be back again before long," she warned the saleswoman as she left the shop.

It was after five by then, and the traffic exiting the city was horrendous. What had been only about a thirty-five-minute drive that morning took almost twice as long in late afternoon, making it close to half past six before she finally arrived on Dimitrios's doorstep a second time.

Erika answered the door. "We were beginning to think you were lost," she said, her glance suggesting she'd have been just as glad if that had been the case. "Dimitrios has been waiting well over an hour for you to show up."

"What for? You told me yesterday that he always spends the evening with Poppy at the hospital."

"As a rule, I do," he said rather curtly, emerging from what appeared to be some sort of library to the right of the front door, "but I thought you might like to come with me tonight, seeing that your visit was cut short this morning. Since you've been out all afternoon, though, you're probably too tired and would rather not bother."

"I'm not in the least bit tired. As for seeing her again, I'd love to, because I went shopping and bought her a gift."

"That's thoughtful of you, Brianna," he said, his tone softening slightly, "but we're pretty restricted on what we can take in."

"I know," she said. "Noelle explained all about that, but look, this will be acceptable, don't you think?" Carefully, she unwrapped the music box and held it up for his inspection. "See, it even has a glass dome covering it that can easily be cleaned, and if it was put someplace where Poppy could see it but not touch it…? Then there's this mobile. I thought it might hang near the window where it would catch the sunlight. What do you think?"

"They might work," he allowed, "and there's no question but that she'd get a kick out of them. You obviously went to a great deal of trouble to find something she'd really enjoy."

"Which is a lot more than the other one would have done," Erika muttered grudgingly. "Will you be back for dinner, Dimitrios?"

"Yes." He glanced at Brianna again. "How hungry are you? Can you hold off until about nine, or would you like a snack before we leave?"

"I can wait."

"Then let's get going, or Poppy'll be asleep before we arrive."

He hustled her outside, not to the Mercedes, as she'd expected—it, along with Spiros, had disappeared again—but to a low-slung black sports car built for comfort and speed. Erika watched them leave, her expression stony with disapproval.

"That woman doesn't like me," Brianna observed, as both housekeeper and villa disappeared from view.

Zooming past the gates that marked the boundary of his estate, Dimitrios made a sharp turn to the road and shifted into high gear. "You can't blame her. You remind her of Cecily."

"Well, if she had an ounce of brains…!" Annoyed with herself, because this was an irritation she'd lived with all her life and she ought to be over it by now, Brianna abruptly halted in midsentence.

"Please don't stop now," he urged, not taking his eyes off the road. "Get it off your chest, whatever it is."

"All right. Cecily and I were two individuals who happened to look alike, but too many people, including you, seem to believe we were—are—interchangeable."

"I soon learned differently. To my cost, I might add."

"And that's another thing! I know better than anyone that Cecily had her faults, but I'm getting sick and tired of hearing other people criticize her. Regardless of what she did or didn't do, she was still my sister. More to the point, she was Poppy's mother, and for that reason alone she deserves a modicum of respect, because no child should have to grow up never hearing a kind word about the woman who gave birth to her. You might be glad Cecily's out of your life, Dimitrios, but I was deeply saddened by her death. Believe it or not, there was a time when she was sweet and kind and loving."

"Before Crete, you mean?"

"No," Brianna admitted, quelling a sigh. "Her decline began long before then. The pity of it was, I didn't recognize it soon enough to put a stop to it."

He spared her a swift glance. "Just yesterday, you told me not to blame myself for the way she ended up. I suggest you take your own advice. And for the record, I did my best to be a good husband, Brianna, and I would never criticize Cecily to Poppy. I tried to make it work between us, if for no other reason than that I don't deal well with failure. It's not in my nature to accept defeat."

"Because you're a control freak," she said.

"Maybe I am, but one thing I learned the hard way is that even I can't control love. I couldn't conjure it up on command, and in all truth, I'm not sure it would have made any difference if I had been able to. You probably don't want to hear this either, but the fact is, Cecily wasn't looking for a husband, she was looking for a meal ticket."

"And what were you looking for, Dimitrios?"

"You," he said candidly. "I was looking for you. And by the time I realized the carbon copy didn't measure up to the original, the damage was done. Now I'm looking for ways to undo it."

She wasn't sure how to respond to that remark, and he didn't seem inclined to elaborate. "Well, at least you have Poppy," she finally said.

"And I thank God for that every day. But what do you have, Brianna? Is there someone special in your life?"

Not about to confess she'd practically lived like a nun since their breakup, she said, "I wouldn't say 'special,' no. My work and the amount of traveling it involves isn't exactly conducive to a long-term commitment."

"So the career *does* takes precedence over all else."

The edge of scorn in his voice was unmistakable. "If it did," she replied hotly, "I wouldn't be here now, would I?"

He shrugged. "Possibly not."

"There's no 'possibly' about it! Maybe I couldn't save my sister from self-destructing, but I'm not about to stand by and watch her daughter die if I can do something to prevent it."

"So what are you saying? That you're here out of guilt or a sense of obligation?"

"Perhaps in the beginning. But certainly not now."

"Why? What's changed in the past twenty-four hours?"

"Everything," she said. "I've fallen in love with my niece."

"For how long? Until she's healthy again, at which point you'll disappear from the canvas and that'll be the last we see of you?"

Was this love-hate pendulum what he meant by a truce? If so, she wanted no part of it. "That is *not* what I said. Stop putting words in my mouth."

"Then what, exactly, are your intentions?"

She gave an involuntary chirp of laughter. "For heaven's sake, Dimitrios, you're not interviewing a prospective suitor."

His lips twitched in an answering smile. An unfortunate response, she decided, hastily looking away. His mouth was a seduction in itself, and when it came to making love, he knew how to use it. And that was definitely not something she wished to be reminded of, especially not when she was trapped beside him in the intimate confines of his car. "I'm going to make a hell of a father-in-law, aren't I?" he said.

"I hope so," she replied, sobering. "With all my heart, I hope we're both going to see the day that Poppy walks down the aisle, a beautiful bride."

"You plan on being there for that, as well, do you?"

"Count on it. I can't take her mother's place, but I can and will do the next best thing."

"I'll hold you to that," he said.

They'd reached Kifissia by then, and the streets were just coming to life as dusk fell. The aroma of roasting meat and garlic and hot olive oil drifted from the open doors of tavernas, displacing the lingering scent of Penteli's pine-drenched air. Groups of people sat outside, their laughter and conversation vying with the music of the bouzouki players wandering among the tables.

Gradually, though, the noise diminished, muffled by the trees lining the streets, and when Dimitrios at last turned onto the steep crescent where the clinic stood and pulled up in the forecourt, a hush hung over the land. Stepping out of the car, Brianna caught the faint whiff of some sweet-smelling night flower. Palm trees swathed the parking area in dense shadow. Overhead, the sky had turned a soft violet. Although the hospital windows glowed softly in the encroaching dark, the raucous noise and bustle and bright lights of Athens might have been a continent away, instead of just a few miles.

They found Poppy almost asleep, but at the sight of Dimitrios, she climbed up and reached for him over the high rails of her bed. "Papa!" she whimpered.

Scooping her into his arms, he paced the room with her, all the while crooning softly in her ear. Eventually she grew quiet. Her little fist relaxed, its fingers spreading like pale petals against his tanned neck. Her head drooped against his chest. Her eyes fell closed. And Brianna had to turn away, so affected by the sight that her heart ached as if squeezed in a vise.

Quietly she left the room. Now was not the time for a stranger bearing gifts to intrude on such a special moment. Nothing money could buy held a candle to the bond between this big, strong man and his tiny, fragile daughter. Leaving the music box and mobile on a table next to her purse in the anteroom, she walked to the window and stared unseeingly at the gardens below.

She didn't turn when she heard him leave Poppy's room. She didn't want him to see the tears clinging to her eyelashes. But, joining her, he noticed anyway. Without a word he put his arms around her and drew her to him. The last time he'd done that, handling her as tenderly as if she were made of spun glass, had been with the murmured promise of a future together.

This time all he said was, "I know."

"Does it ever get easier," she asked, when she was able to speak again. "Coming here and seeing her so alone and ill, I mean?"

"No. But you get used to the pain."

"I don't think I will. I'm not strong like you."

"You'd be surprised, Brianna, at how much a parent will endure to help his child."

Not very much in my sister's case, she thought sadly, shaken by a sob she couldn't stifle. It was all very fine to lay the blame for Cecily's behavior at someone else's feet, but the fact remained, she'd left her baby to be brought up by a housekeeper, and shown such disregard for her own life that it ended before her daughter had laid down any lasting memories of the woman who'd brought her into the world. What sort of legacy was that?

"Enough now," Dimitrios scolded. "I'm taking you home. Poppy's asleep for the night and you're exhausted. Tomorrow's Saturday. We'll come back in the morning when she's more alert and you can give her your gifts then."

Still with his arm around her waist, they left the clinic.

Soon enough, they'd left Kifissia, too, and were following the twisting mountain road back to Rafina. "Doesn't it bother you, having to drive so far to see her?" Brianna asked, breaking a silence which had lasted almost fifteen minutes.

"No. I like being on the coast. Sailing's one of my passions—at least, it used to be, when I had the time and inclination to enjoy it. And it's better for Poppy to grow up away from the city. The air pollution in Athens grows worse every year."

"Did Cecily like Rafina?"

He let out a soft snort of laughter. "What do *you* think, Brianna?"

"She might have found it a little…isolated."

"She loathed it," he said, "although for the first year she pretended it was just what she wanted. But toward the end, she spent hardly any time there at all."

Puzzled, she said, "Where did she go?"

"I had an apartment in the city, in Kolonaki, which I've since sold. She stayed there."

"Alone? She didn't take Poppy with her?"

"She didn't take Poppy. And she wasn't alone."

Shocked speechless by the implication in his words, she stared at him.

"That's right," he said. "She had company. Of the male kind."

"Why didn't you divorce her?"

"I didn't care enough to bother. I—"

The car, until then purring smoothly along the unfolding ribbon of road like a sleek, well-bred cat, suddenly rebelled. For no apparent reason, the engine simply gave up the ghost. The only sound to break the silence was the soft hiss of the tires, and Dimitrios cursing as he wrestled with the steering wheel.

Somehow, before it lost all forward momentum, he managed to bring the vehicle to the shoulder of the highway and set the emergency brake. "Son of a bitch!" he remarked pleasantly.

"What happened?"

"Well, I'm not out of gas, so that eliminates one possibility." He dimmed the headlamps but pressed a button on the dash. "And the hazard lights work, which suggests the problem isn't electrical, so my guess is some other computer part has failed. Not that I pretend to be any sort of auto mechanic, you understand."

"So what do we do now?"

"I call Spiros to come and collect us." Lifting the car phone from its cradle, he accessed the number, spoke briefly, and hung up. "Done. Ten minutes, fifteen tops, and we'll home."

"What about this car?"

He angled his body toward her and slung a casual arm over the back of her seat. The blinking yellow hazard lights made him appear more shadow than substance, but the heat of his body was very, very real. "It'll be towed in for repair."

"I see." She cleared her throat, all too aware of the solitude of their situation. The last house they'd passed lay several kilometers behind them. "So what do we do until Spiros gets here?"

"We wait." His voice grazed her ear. His warm breath drifted over her face. "And pass the time the best way we know how."

Her lungs just about seized up on her. "I don't think we should be doing this, Dimitrios," she protested feebly.

"Why not? If you were telling me the truth earlier, I'm not poaching on another man's territory."

Blink, blink, blink went the hazard lights, regular as a heart monitor. Except her heart wasn't keeping time. It was leaping around behind her ribs like a mad thing. And other parts of her, parts well below her waist, were stirring in ways that left her taut with forbidden delight.

"Perhaps not, but the fact remains, you're my brother-in-law," she gasped, turning her face aside and pushing him away with one hand. Big mistake! He was all firm, heated masculine flesh and steely muscle beneath his shirt.

He placed his forefinger at the side of her jaw and effortlessly turned her face to his again. "And now I'm a widower. By my reckoning, that frees both of us to listen to our hearts. I can't speak for yours, *karthula mou,* but mine is telling me this is long overdue."

His mouth nudged hers, masterful, persuasive, and no

amount of frantic rationalizing on her part could turn it into a brotherly peck. His hands shaped her face, mapping every curve, every hollow, with the minute attention to detail of a blind man.

"Why don't we stop pretending we don't know where this is leading?" he murmured.

She wished she could tell him it wasn't going anywhere, but the inescapable fact remained that what was happening had slipped right off the friendship scale and veered altogether too close to love of the man-and-woman, Adam-and-Eve kind. He was blatantly, flagrantly, seducing her. Sending time spinning backward. Reviving old yearnings and leaving them screaming for satisfaction.

His fingers stroked down her neck, dipped inside the top of her blouse, close enough to bring her nipples surging to life, but not enough that she could actually accuse him of fondling her breasts.

He was stealing her soul. Making her forget she was supposed to hate him. She should have slapped him. Jumped out of the car and waited on the road for Spiros to rescue her. Instead she melted. Enthralled past all reason, she cast off any thought of self-preservation. The kind of magic he wove was too rare, too blissful, to resist. He reminded her of things she'd ignored for a very long time; in particular that, beneath her glossy exterior, she was a very lonely woman who'd been aching and empty for far too long.

Her hand slid up his chest to his neck. Her fingers tangled in his hair. She clung to him, her body yearning toward him, a moan of raw need rising in her throat. If the console separating their two seats hadn't made it virtually impossible, she'd have climbed into his lap.

The blaze of approaching headlights cut across the scene, a timely interruption that snapped her back to reality before she made a complete fool of herself. Oh, she was hopeless, pathetic, to have succumbed so quickly, so easily, to temptation.

"Thank God!" she breathed, recognizing Spiros at the wheel of the Mercedes as it made a U-turn in the road and came to a stop behind them. She groped for her purse lying at her feet and made a grab for the door handle in her haste to get away from Dimitrios.

But at the last minute he reached over and stopped her. "Run as far and as fast as you like, Brianna, but what just started here isn't finished, not by a long shot."

"Nothing started," she panted.

"You think not, *karthula mou?*" he inquired, his own breathing as ragged as hers. "Then I suggest you think again."

CHAPTER SIX

DINNER turned into an onerous affair. The conversation was stilted, the atmosphere charged with tension, the superbly presented butterflied scampi and chilled white wine flavored equally with sexual awareness and disapproval.

Brianna sat across from Dimitrios with what seemed like an acre of table separating him from her. A safe enough distance, she'd have thought. But its glass top unfortunately provided him with an unimpaired view of every inch of her, from the tip of her black sandals to the top of her head. If she crossed her ankles, he noticed. If she tugged at her skirt or scratched her knee, he saw.

"You don't seem to be enjoying your meal, Brianna," he remarked, watching as she rearranged the food on her plate. "Why not? I know how much you like shellfish."

"You do?"

"Of course," he said, his lazy gaze traveling the length of her and back again. "I remember everything about you."

No doubt including the fact that she'd been a virgin when she met him and hadn't known an orgasm from an aubergine!

He'd wasted no time teaching her the difference, and if

his scrutiny now was any indication, seemed bent on fur-
thering her education as soon as possible. His camera eyes
captured everything they saw and recorded it in the steel
trap that was his mind. Smoldering eyes that burned
through her clothes and seared her flesh.

At the other end of the spectrum, Erika stood in the
corner, vengeful as a crow in her severe black blouse and
ankle-length skirt. Ready to defend him should he come
under attack, she kept her cold, beady gaze fixed accus-
ingly on Brianna. With good reason, because Brianna
hadn't merely submitted to his overtures in the car, she'd
responded to them willingly. Eagerly. And she knew her
cheeks glowed like neon signs advertising her guilty secret
for all the world to see.

Not that it was any of Erika's business.

*She acts as if she's his mother and I'm some hussy
who's set her sights on him,* Brianna thought balefully.
*What does she think? That I pinned him down in the back
seat of the Mercedes and had my way with him when Spiros
wasn't looking?*

Finally even Dimitrios had had enough of his housekeeper's surveillance. "*Efharisto,* Erika, that'll be all," he
said, after the main course had been cleared away and
coffee served. "We can manage by ourselves now."

With one last inimical glare at Brianna, the woman
departed, leaving behind a silence so fraught with electricity that it was almost worse than her hovering presence. A
minute passed. Stretched to two, then three. Dimitrios
rested his elbow on the upholstered arm of his chair,
stretched out his long legs, and continued his leisurely observation.

Schooling herself not to fidget, Brianna scoured her

mind for some pithy conversational gambit that might distract him, but "Lovely weather we're having," didn't quite cut it. So, reminding herself of the adage that it was better to keep her mouth shut and be thought a fool, than to open it and remove all doubt, she focused her attention on the dancing candle flames reflected in the table top. And still the silence stretched, taut as a bow string.

At last, when she was about ready to drain her glass of wine in one gulp, then do the same to the bottle, he said, "You're upset."

"My goodness," she retorted acidly, "how did you guess?"

"With me?"

The temptation to lie and say "yes" nagged at her, but there'd been enough untruths in the mess between them, and even if she was willing to deceive him, she refused to deceive herself. "No. With me."

"Why? Because I kissed you and touched you, and you couldn't deny it's exactly what you wanted me to do?"

That, and a whole lot more than she cared to admit. But the real problem was less easily defined because he touched her in other ways that had nothing to do with the physical. "No," she confessed. "Because I'm in danger of repeating a mistake which cost me dearly the first time around, and that's something I promised myself I wouldn't let happen a second time."

"What mistake is that?"

"That once again, I'm on the point of leaping headfirst into an involvement with you, without considering the risks."

"What if I were to tell you there are no risks this time? That all I want is to put right what went wrong between us before, and pick up where we left off?"

Desperately trying to shore up her crumbling defenses, she said, "You didn't give me that impression yesterday. You were openly hostile."

"Perhaps I was, at first. But then…" He didn't exactly sigh; he wasn't that kind of man. Instead he exhaled and gave a shrug that drew her attention to his broad shoulders. "Since we're talking truth at all costs, I admit I was looking to find flaws in you where once I'd seen only perfection. I hoped you'd changed, that you were beginning to lose your looks and had nothing underneath. No warmth, no heart, no humanity. I hoped that the giving, passionate woman I fell in love with really was nothing more than the cold-blooded tease I had reason to believe she'd become, and that seeing you again would reinforce what I'd been telling myself for years: that I was well rid of you."

"Well, in a way, you got your wish because the plain fact is, I'm not the same as I was when we first met, and nor are you," she pointed out. "Life happened, Dimitrios, and it's changed us. We can't go back to the way we once were, any more than a smashed china plate can be glued back together without showing any cracks. So what's the point of pretending otherwise?"

"The point," he said, "is that, despite everything, it's not too late for us. We're not china plates, we're two intelligent, consenting adults with no ties to other partners. To the best of my knowledge, nowhere is it written that as such, we're not entitled to a second chance."

This wasn't part of the plan. In fact, it was in direct contradiction to everything she'd resolved. He was part of her past, and not one overflowing with happy memories. Yet his kiss in the car, and now the way he was looking at her, and the tone of his voice—somehow they were managing to erase all that old, tired grief and revive a joy and anticipation she'd only ever experienced with him.

Schooling herself to caution, she said, "I rather think the only reason you feel that way is that you're facing a terribly difficult situation, and it would help if you weren't doing it alone."

"I'm not alone, Brianna, and if all I need is support, I can find it in my large network of friends, and a household of loyal staff."

"I didn't mean…that kind of alone."

"You think I've lived like a monk since Cecily died?" His mouth curved in bitter amusement. "I might be widowed, *koritsi mou,* but I've still got a pulse. If all I want is sex, I don't have to import it from North America."

"Then why are you pursuing me? You already know I'll do whatever I can to help Poppy."

"You know why, Brianna. Because we belong together and we always have. Do I want to make love to you? Of course I do, badly enough that I'd take you right here on this table, if you were willing. But you're not so naive as to think a relationship is only about sex. And *that's* the point I'm trying to make. I want a relationship. Not just any relationship, but one with you."

"Would you still be talking this way if I told you I've decided against going ahead with the tests? That I've changed my mind about becoming a donor for Poppy?"

"But you haven't," he said. "And you won't. You're not that kind of person, which is another reason I'm falling for you all over again."

"What if it turns out that I'm not a suitable match?"

"Then we'll keep looking for someone who is. And if I have my way, we'll do it together. I can't keep you here against your will, and if your career matters too much to give it up, I'll let you go. But I'm warning you now, I won't make it easy for you. I'll do my damnedest to make you want to stay."

One by one he was systematically destroying every barrier she'd erected against him. Beset on all sides, she buried her face in her hands, not knowing which way to turn. Her career wasn't the issue. She could kiss that goodbye and never miss it if, in its place, she found true love and fulfillment as a wife and a mother.

But desire, passion, yearning? How did she subdue their voracious demands and relegate them to their proper place? How separate them from the more enduring dimensions of a relationship, like friendship and trust and common values? Heaven knew, the temptation to cast caution to the winds and fling herself into an affair with him was strong. But if, once their carnal appetites were satisfied, she found there was nothing of substance left, what then? How would she survive losing him a second time?

She heard his chair scrape back, felt him gently prying her hands away so that he could look her in the eye. "You don't have to give me an answer now," he said. "I won't pretend I'm a patient man because I'm not. When I want something badly enough, I go after it with all I've got. And make no mistake about it, Brianna. I want and need you in every way a man can want and need a woman. Four years ago, I recognized you as my soul mate and it's taken no time at all for me to realize that's still the case. But until you decide you feel the same way about me, I won't press you for an answer. All I ask is that you give some unbiased thought to the idea of us as a couple, and know that my feelings for you aren't going to change, no matter what your final decision might be."

"And in the meantime?"

"Oh, I'm not going to make it easy for you," he admitted, beguiling her with his smile. "I never said I'd be content to sit on my hands and not take action. I intend to woo you at every turn. But tonight, I'll settle for this."

He drew her to her feet and tilted up her chin with his thumb. His eyes, their irises dark gray ringed with black, their lashes casting a dense inky shadow in the candlelight, tracked her face, feature by feature.

His lips followed, sampling the hollow beneath her cheekbones, the corner of her jaw, the bridge of her nose. His mouth flirted with hers but never quite settled, a feast for her starving soul, cruelly held just beyond reach.

The last of her resistance in tatters, she clutched fistfuls of his shirt front. "Dimitrios," she begged, the persistent throb of frustrated desire tormenting her.

He traced the outline of her mouth with his fingertip. Slid it between her parted lips and out again, a boldly unmistakable promise made more erotic by the urgent thrust of his flesh which neither his slim-fitting trousers nor the silky fabric of her dress could disguise.

Heaven alone knew what she might not have done or said next, had his cell phone not interrupted the moment. "Under any other circumstances," he muttered, his breathing almost as strangled as hers, "I would ignore this, but with Poppy…"

"I understand."

"I know you do." Flipping open the phone, he glanced at the display screen and turned pale beneath his tan. Tonelessly, he said, "It's Noelle."

Brianna's heart missed a beat, and far from escaping when opportunity presented itself, as had been her original intention, she stood rooted to the spot. The hands of a marble wall clock showed seventeen minutes after ten. At that hour, whatever the reason for the doctor's call, it couldn't be good.

Dimitrios paced the length of the room to the glass doors opening onto the terrace, the phone clamped to his ear. "No," Brianna heard him say. "We're just finishing dinner. What…? Oh, that! With everything that's happened lately…no, of course I haven't forgotten, it just got pushed to the back of my mind…. I haven't asked her, but either way, I'm still depending on you to be there, Noelle…. Don't be silly, I'm always available to speak to you, you know that. Absolutely…. Good night."

He slapped the phone closed and turned back into the room, his face the picture of relief.

"I take it Poppy's fine?" Brianna ventured.

"Yes." He shook his head ruefully. "I'm not sure I am, though. First, I forget an important business meeting this morning, one that had been arranged months ago. And now, another couple of important dates have crept up without my realizing. See the effect you have on me?"

"Dates?"

"If you can call them that, yes, though they're as much a social obligation as anything. I offered my place as the venue for a garden party being held next Sunday to honor the people who've supported the Rosegarth with private donations throughout the year. The annual fund-raising gala that is open to the general public takes place the following Saturday. I always support both, but this year's events hold special significance for me, as you can imagine. If it weren't for the generosity of other people, there'd be no clinic here in Athens and I'd have had to take Poppy to another country for treatment."

"And you'll have Noelle for moral support both times. That's nice."

She thought she'd done a pretty good job of hiding the unreasonable burst of jealousy welling up within her, but something in her voice must have given her away because he skewered her in a sharp glance. "She agreed to stand in as hostess next weekend, yes, and I offered to be her escort at the gala. I made these plans weeks ago, before I knew you'd be here, but in case you're wondering, there's nothing romantic going on between me and Noelle. We've known each other for quite some time, but it's only recently, since her involvement with Poppy, that we've become close friends."

"I see."

"I hope you do," he said, an edge of steel in his words, "because I had my share of emotional game playing with Cecily, and I'm not interested in going another round with you. I don't lie, Brianna, and I don't expect you to lie, either. For what it's worth, Noelle was calling to let me off the hook on both occasions, especially the garden party. But as you won't know many people, I told her to leave things as they stand. I don't see a problem with that, but if you do, I won't press you to attend. For my part, though, I've made a commitment and I intend to keep it."

"I'd like to be there," she said, ashamed. In her own way, she was as much a mass of insecurities as Cecily had been, and for the same reasons. Valued by her mother for her looks and what they earned. The trophy girlfriend, desired by men for her glamour. But until Dimitrios, never loved for herself; for the woman inside the body, the brain behind the face.

"You're sure?"

"Yes. And I'm sorry I responded badly just now. It was a stupid, knee-jerk reaction."

He caught her hands and pulled her to him. "Old habits die hard, and we've both been burned. But sweetheart, dragging all that old baggage with us will kill any chance we have of a successful future together."

"You're right, but sometimes that's easier said than done." She leaned against him. Felt the strong, unhurried beat of his heart. Everything he said made sense, so why was it, now that they'd cleared up the misunderstandings of the past, that she persisted in looking for flaws? "You know, Dimitrios, for all that I've defended her to you, I'm still having a hard time getting past what Cecily did. I knew she resented me at some level, but I had no idea she'd take it that far."

"*Mana mou,* I don't say this to hurt you, but Cecily resented anyone she perceived as having more than she did, whether it was to do with money or business or relationships. No matter how much you gave her, how much she already had, it was never enough. She couldn't stand knowing someone else might have more. That was reason enough for her to try to take it away and keep it for herself."

Deep down Brianna knew that to be true. "You're right again," she said bleakly. "I guess I just haven't wanted to admit it."

"You always gave her the benefit of the doubt. It's what families do for one another. And that's why it cuts so deep when family betrays you. Trust me, I ought to know."

"What do you mean?"

His expression changed. Grew guarded; forbidding almost. "It's a long story that can wait for another day. Go to bed, Brianna. You look worn-out."

He went to drop a kiss on her cheek, but just as the fragments in a kaleidoscope could assume a different pattern with the merest twist of the wrist, so her connection with him underwent swift change. In the brief second before he'd masked it, she'd glimpsed pain in his eyes, and a loneliness that matched her own.

Unable to help herself, she cradled his face and turned it so that their parted lips met. And meshed. And lingered.

At first he resisted. Held her firmly by the shoulders and tried to step away. But his determination was no match for hers. She wrapped her arms around his waist, hung on tight and refused to let him go.

He tasted of coffee and wine and sexual hunger kept severely in check; a potent aphrodisiac that shot straight to her bloodstream and surged through her veins like wildfire. With an inarticulate whisper, she sank against him, pressing her breasts to the solid plane of his chest and tilting her hips so that her body nested against his where he was most susceptible.

He almost weakened. His hand slid down her spine to cup her bottom and hold her hard and fast. His fingers plucked at her skirt, inching it high enough to give him access to the smooth bare skin of her thigh.

She felt a shock of damp warmth at her core. A trembling weakness in her limbs. An aching in her breasts. A bone-deep hunger that had waited years too long for satisfaction.

And then it was over. Cool night air replaced the heat of his mouth, his hands. "I'm trying my utmost to do the decent thing and abide by your rules," he ground out savagely, "but if you persist with this, I'm going to take you right here on the floor, and if you wake up tomorrow full of regret, you'll have only yourself to blame."

"I thought you wanted me," she quavered.

"I've always wanted you, Brianna, and not just because I desire you sexually. I want you in my life and in my daughter's. I want you to wear my ring and bear my children. In other words, *khriso mou,* I'm in this for the long haul. When you can tell me you feel the same way, we'll make love, but not before."

She bit her lip, humiliated. "I don't make a habit of throwing myself at men."

"That's good to know, because I'd break the neck of any man I saw as competition, and I don't relish the idea of spending the rest of my life behind bars. Greek prisons aren't known for their creature comforts." He turned her around and gave her a smart swat on the behind. "I'll see you at breakfast. Now get to bed before my baser instincts get the better of me."

In the week following, they established a routine that allowed them to take care of business, maintain an uninterrupted schedule of visits with Poppy and still leave enough time for their unhurried rediscovery of each other.

Each day, he drove them both into the city and dropped Brianna off at the clinic where she spent sweet, tranquil hours with her niece. Sometimes she read to her, or sang, or wound up the music box, or set the mobile in motion. Other times she'd carry her to the window and they'd wave to people in the gardens below and wait for Dimitrios's car to turn into the forecourt. And sometimes, she'd simply sit and watch her as she slept, and pray that she'd be able to save this precious child's life.

Whenever they could steal time for themselves, Dimitrios showed her Athens. Not just the popular sights, but places the tourists seldom discovered. Tiny tavernas tucked away behind bougainvillea-draped walls, that served wonderful intimate dinners by candlelight. Narrow streets lined with ateliers full of exquisite paintings and sculptures by little-known artists who loved what they created more than they cared about fame and fortune. Out-of-the-way little churches in dusty squares, where old women knelt on their bony knees and prayed for their dead husbands and new-born great-grandchildren.

To preserve the privacy she and Dimitrios treasured, Brianna hid behind large concealing sunglasses. With her hair tied back, and her casual skirts and tops and flat-heeled sandals, she blended in with the crowd, another un-remarkable woman wandering the city with her man. Only once did a photographer recognize her, and Dimitrios made short work of him.

One morning, he took her to his corporate headquarters, just off Syntagma Square, and introduced her to his col-leagues. Not surprisingly, that day she caused a stir.

"Did you see their faces?" she exclaimed, afterward.

"They'd better get used to it, is all I can say, because if I have my way, they'll be seeing a lot more of you."

They were alone in the elevator at the time, and he seized the opportunity to back her up against the padded leather wall and kiss her so thoroughly that she turned liquid with pleasure.

If the warning *ping!* of the doors opening to admit another passenger hadn't interrupted the moment, what might have happened next didn't bear thinking about. Bad enough that she was all rosy and breathless, with her nipples visibly advertising their presence under her cotton blouse.

"You're so bad!" she muttered, slipping her sunglasses

in place as they left the building and stepped out into the midday sun.

He grinned unrepentantly. "Small wonder, my dear. The novelty of my self-imposed chastity is taking a terrible toll."

For her, too. His smile, his touch, his kiss, his every glance, filled her with a riot of sensation. She melted in the warmth of his smile. Went weak at the knees when he kissed her. Ached for him in the lonely luxury of her bed.

Yet she worried they were hurtling along at too fast a pace when they should have been taking the time to be sure, *really* sure, they were getting it right this time. Because it was no longer just about the two of them. Poppy was part of the mix, and she'd already lost one mother. She didn't deserve to lose another. No child did.

On the Thursday she met again with Noelle and began the round of preliminary tests at the clinic. For the next two days, she was weighed, measured and X-rayed. Poked and prodded by an endless stream of technicians and doctors who took endless blood samples. Quizzed about everything from her childhood ailments, to her diet, to possible allergies, to her menstrual cycle.

"I warned you we'd be thorough," Noelle said with a smile.

And with every passing hour, Brianna and Dimitrios grew closer. Whatever the interruptions during the day, they always made time to be together last thing at night. Walking the beach after dark, stolen kisses and touches that set her on fire, and hard-won restraint: these formed the foundation of their new understanding, the pattern of their renewal, even though every inch of her body screamed for the ultimate intimacy, the easing of a perpetual ache that only he could bring.

When they'd first met, she'd fallen in love with his cosmopolitan tastes, his sharp intelligence, his wit and charm. She'd been seduced by the deep, exotic purr of his voice, and his masculine beauty. By his passion and sensitivity.

This time she loved him for all that and more. For laying bare all the misunderstandings and lies that had come between them, and for taking the time to court her, just as he'd promised he would. Most of all, though, she loved him for the father he'd become.

He stole her heart with his gentleness with his little girl; with his patience and tenderness. She loved how his big hands cradled Poppy's little body; how he snuggled her against his shoulder. She loved his tone of voice, his face as he watched her sleep, his pain when she cried. Everything to do with his daughter made Brianna want to put her arms around him and give him comfort and support however she could. With her body, her heart, her soul, her life.

Somehow she resisted, knowing it was too soon. There was too much else going on and all of it so steeped in emotion that it was hard to separate sex from stress; empathy from love. She had to be cautious. He'd broken her heart once. She'd never survive his doing it a second time.

"You're going to wear yourself to a shadow worrying about the two of them, if you're not careful," Erika informed reprovingly.

But her words, Brianna noticed, lacked the bite of a week ago. "I can't help it, Erika," she replied. "They both mean too much to me. In any case, you worry, too. I know you do."

"Because I belong with them. But how long before you

grow tired of the whole business and walk out, just like the other one did?"

"I'm not my sister, Erika, and I don't play fast and loose with other people's lives, especially not a child's. I love that little girl as if she were my own."

"Hmm," came the reply on a disparaging sniff. "Time will tell, I suppose."

The next morning, though, she scooped up the last hot breakfast scone and deposited it on Brianna's plate before Dimitrios could reach for it.

"I do believe you're winning her over," he remarked, sotto voce, as the housekeeper went to refill their coffee cups.

From the other side of the breakfast room, Erika said sharply, "I heard that!"

But there was no real sting in her tone. In fact, when she turned back to the table, the hint of a smile played over her mouth.

Moved by the small gesture of acceptance, Brianna realized that this was what real families were all about—affectionate teasing and loyalty and devotion and the willingness to give one another a chance. Why hadn't Cecily recognized the gift she'd been given, and grabbed hold of it with both hands?

Brianna knew why. Because her poor sister had never learned how to love unselfishly. She and Brianna had only ever known the fickle approval of a parent perennially dissatisfied with her lot in life. To their mother, they'd always been either a burden or the means to an end; something she could exploit to her own advantage. If the desired results didn't bring her the rewards she felt she deserved, her children paid the price. And Cecily had continued along the same path with Poppy, showering her with attention when it suited and ignoring her when it didn't.

Well, no more, Brianna decided, as she lay in bed that night. The destructive pattern of behavior ended here.

"I've made my decision, Dimitrios," she announced, the next morning. "About us. And if your offer to make me a permanent part of your life still stands, I'd very much like to see if we can make it work."

CHAPTER SEVEN

HE REGARDED her solemnly. "So soon? Are you sure?"

"Yes, I'm sure."

"You've really thought it through?"

"I've really thought it through," she confirmed, somewhat disconcerted by his measured response. She'd expected a little more enthusiasm. Unbridled ecstasy, even. After all, picking up where they'd left off four years earlier had been his suggestion, not hers.

"In case I haven't made it clear," he said, holding her in his serous gaze, "I'm not looking for an affair. I want you as my wife."

As proposals went, this one left something to be desired, enough that she looked at him blankly, wondering if she hadn't heard him correctly. "Your what?"

"My wife, Brianna. As in *Kyria Dimitrios Giannakis.*"

No mistaking it, this time. He couldn't have made himself any clearer if he'd had it emblazoned in gold on his forehead.

Elation fizzed through her veins, heady as champagne. Dimitrios, her husband? She'd buried that particular dream a long time ago, yet here it was, resurrected from the ashes. A modern-day miracle.

If something sounds too good to be true, Carter's voice whispered in her head, just as it had often enough in the past, *take care, because it probably is. Look for the hidden agenda, Brianna. Don't be so ready to take everything at face value.*

But she turned a deaf ear. He'd been referring to business; to the dog-eat-dog world of international modeling. This was different. This was about matters of the heart. About love and commitment. What for so long had seemed a hopeless fantasy had suddenly turned into a reality, and she wanted to jump up and dance with sheer happiness. She wanted Dimitrios to catch her in his arms and swing her off her feet and smother her in kisses.

Instead he remained seated, spelling out his terms with the uncompromising exactitude he no doubt brought to his corporate acquisitions.

Except…she wasn't a corporate acquisition. Was she?

Her skin prickled as if a cold wind had drafted up her spine. Reining in her initial uprush of delight, she said, "I wouldn't have it any other way, Dimitrios. I'm really not interested in being your live-in mistress."

"You'll be taking on a husband with a ready-made family, not to mention a new country and a whole new life that leaves no room for your celebrity career. I want more children, Brianna, and I expect my wife to be a hands-on mother."

"Well, just in case *I* haven't made it clear to *you,*" she retorted, adopting an equally direct manner, "I consider being a wife and a mother far more of a career than walking the runways of Milan and Paris. But while you might not hold that world in very high regard, let me point out in its defense that it taught me a lot about dedication, patience, and self-discipline. As I see it, they're qualities which should meet your exacting standards at the same time that they stand me in very good stead as a wife and mother."

His beautiful, sexy mouth twitched. "Yes, ma'am! If I spoke out of turn, consider me well and truly chastised."

"Furthermore," she went on, really hitting her stride, "marriage is a contract between equals, not a favor conferred by one party on the other. Marrying you won't make me your chattel, Dimitrios, it'll make me your partner."

"I agree. I just want you to be sure you can live with my expectations. I settled for less than I wanted with Cecily. I won't settle again. One failed marriage is enough. I want you to be happy, Brianna, but—"

"There's no doubt in my mind that in becoming your wife and Poppy's mother, I'd be gaining far more than I'd be giving up," she said, torn between understanding and resentment. "Far more, in fact, than I ever dared dream about or hope for. I've only ever loved one man, Dimitrios, and that man is you. But if that's not enough to convince you that I know what I'm getting myself into, then perhaps you're the one who's not sure."

His dark eyes gleamed with amusement. "Oh, I've never been more certain of anything my entire life. But I feel obligated to point out that I can be difficult. Some might even say high-handed."

"How about downright bossy, not to mention arrogant?"

"I'm Greek. It's the nature of the beast, at least in my case."

"I've noticed."

"You think you can handle me?"

"About as well as you can handle me, which is to say it'll be enough of a challenge that life will never be dull."

At that, he broke into a smile that took her breath away.

His gaze softened. Grew dark with emotion. He pushed his chair back from the table so abruptly it crashed to the tiled floor. "Come here, woman," he ordered, his voice rich as molasses, and hauled her into his arms. "This bossy, arrogant Greek wants to kiss his bride."

He did. At very great length, and with all the fire and passion she could ask for.

Later that morning as they drove the familiar streets of Kifissia to the clinic, he mentioned that a catering crew would be spending the day at the villa, setting up for tomorrow's event.

She laughed. "You mean to say Erika and Alexio are going to let strangers run loose all over the place?"

"They oversee everything, but it's too big an affair for them to manage by themselves. To give them a break, we'll have dinner in Rafina tonight."

"Why?" she objected. "I don't mind cooking, and I'm happy to spend a quiet evening at home with you."

"That's the whole point. It won't be quiet, and the kitchen will be off-limits."

"Oh, I hadn't thought of that. Well, just for the record, you don't have to wine and dine me every night of the week."

He grimaced slightly. "Keep reminding me of that, will you? It's not something I'm used to."

"Cecily needed constant entertainment, I know."

"Oh, yeah. And if I wasn't able or willing to provide it, she went looking for someone who was."

"You never told me who was with her, the night she died."

"Nobody I knew. They might have been part of her new circle of friends, or perfect strangers. She wasn't choosy about the company she kept when it came time to party.

The police report stated only that there'd been a fire in a night club and she was among those who hadn't made it out alive, most likely because, as the autopsy showed, she'd consumed enough alcohol to put someone twice her size under the table."

"It'll be different with us, Dimitrios. I know most people think a model's life is all about wearing fabulous clothes and flying first class from one exotic location to another, but in my case at least, the truth is somewhat different. I'm a real homebody at heart, and never more content than when I can shut my front door on the rest of the world, put on a comfortable old pair of sweatpants, and curl up by the fire with a good book."

"Don't," he said roughly. "Don't make me regret the years I've wasted with you any more than I already do."

"We'll make up for them. We've already started."

He reached over and squeezed her hand. "I guess we have. But speaking of work, do you have outstanding assignments to complete or contracts you need to honor?"

"As a matter of fact, I don't. Carter managed to get someone else to stand in for the work I had coming up, and we were planning to look over some new offers when I went home, but as far as I'm concerned, the only thing I plan to sign in the near future is the consent form for the transplant. Speaking of which, do you have any idea when we'll get my test results?"

"Later in the week, according to Noelle. Listen, Brianna, if you turn out to be a match and the transplant goes ahead, you realize what it means, don't you? You'll be back on your feet in about a week, but Poppy's going to take months to recuperate."

"I know, and I'm sick at the thought of what she faces."

"Me, too. But what I'm getting at is that it's taken me a long time to find my way back to you. Will you think me very selfish if I ask you to marry me as soon possible?"

"How soon is that?"

He turned into the clinic forecourt and killed the engine. "You're not a Greek citizen, so there'll be some red tape to cut through, but I have connections in all the right places that can speed up the process. I'd say we could set a date for a couple of weeks from now. We'd have to postpone the honeymoon, obviously, but the wedding itself can be anything you want."

"I want you." She swiveled in her seat and let her gaze roam over him. She'd never tire of looking at him, she thought dreamily. Nothing time could affect would lessen the perfect bone structure that blessed him with such elegantly sculpted features. Even in old age, he'd be beautiful. "You and Poppy," she said, curving her hand over his thigh. "All the rest is just window dressing."

"Stop that," he scolded, removing her hand and dropping it firmly in her own lap. "I'm a well-respected corporate giant in these parts, not some hormone-driven teenager with an overload of testosterone. Much more temptation of the kind you're dishing out, though, and I won't be responsible for my actions."

"And here I thought you couldn't wait to have at me." She sighed in mock regret. "How long must I wait?"

Choking back a laugh, he glanced at his watch. "About another twelve hours or so, if it's up to me. But regardless of when, I guarantee it'll be someplace a lot more comfortable and private than the passenger seat in my car. Now take my mind off your delicious body and tell me what you have planned for the rest of the day."

"I thought I'd be with you and Poppy."

"I hoped so, too, but a client I've been trying to hook up with for a while now is in Athens just for the day, before he flies to the Orient, which means there'll be no spiriting you away for a romantic lunch while Poppy takes her nap."

"In that case, I might go shopping. You've probably noticed I didn't bring many clothes with me. This sort of thing…" She indicated her plain white cotton skirt and silk-screened T-shirt. "The quality might be good, but it was never intended for a high-society garden party, but I saw something in a boutique the other day that would be perfect. I think you'll like it."

The look he turned on her made her quiver inside. "Haven't you figured out yet that what's inside the clothes is all that matters to me?"

"Still, the last thing I want is to embarrass you in front of your friends and associates."

"Brianna, *mana mou,* you couldn't embarrass me if you tried." Stopping her as she went to open the car door, he leaned over and dropped a kiss on her cheek. "That's for Poppy, and this—" he kissed her again, a lovely, hot, open-mouthed kiss that sent shock waves of delight shimmering all the way to the soles of her feet "—is for you. Consider it a down payment on what I owe you. Have fun shopping, treat yourself to a nice, relaxed lunch, and I'll see you later."

She didn't immediately go up to Poppy's room after he left. She went instead to sit by the courtyard fountain, wanting to savor the moment and let the taste of joy linger on her tongue. How different everything looked through the eyes of a woman in love. The sky reflected a deeper, more intense blue, the flowers a more brilliant palette of scarlet and purple and gold, the lawns a richer shade of emerald. If she was able to make Poppy well again, all truly would be right with the world.

The dress—*her* dress—was still in the window when she arrived at the boutique just ahead of the siesta hour, but recognizing her from a magazine spread she'd done in Paris earlier in the year, the owner, Elene, was more than happy to hang a Closed sign on the door and accommodate her.

"Thavmasios!" she gushed, rolling her eyes dramatically when Brianna emerged from the fitting room in a swirl of pale roses and fine silk voile. "Not many women have the height and body to carry such an ensemble, but on you, Despinis Connelly, it is perfection."

Turning slowly before the three-way mirror to get a better view of how she looked from the back, Brianna had to agree. The entire outfit might have been made with her in mind. The draped bodice molded softly to her shoulders and breasts. The skirt fell in graceful folds from its high empire waist almost to her ankles. The hat was nothing less than a work of art. Its wide sweeping brim, anchored to the crown with one large, perfect cream satin rose, imparted a demure air of mystery to her face. Even the high-heeled ivory shoes were the correct size.

"You are pleased?" Elene eyed her anxiously.

"More than you can begin to imagine," Brianna assured her. "I fell in love with this dress over a week ago, and was afraid it might have sold before I came back. It's one of a kind, I'm sure."

"Indeed, yes. Everything you see here is unique. You needn't concern yourself that you'll come across a duplicate on someone else. But if you are undecided, I have other designs I can show you."

"I decided the minute I saw it. It's perfect for the garden party I'm attending tomorrow. But I would like to look at a few other things, in particular something suitable for evening. Next weekend, I'm also going to the Rosegarth Clinic fund-raising gala. Perhaps you know of it?"

Elene nodded energetically. "Everybody in Athens knows of it, and you're right, it is a very chic, sophisticated affair. I have had a steady stream of clients coming here, hoping to find just the right gown. Please slip into a kimono, make yourself comfortable, and enjoy a glass of champagne while I bring out a few items for your consideration."

Some forty minutes later, Brianna climbed into a taxi, loaded down with an assortment of gorgeous items tenderly wrapped in tissue paper and secured with ribbon in shiny black shopping bags and boxes bearing the boutique's discreet silver logo. She had her evening gown, her garden party outfit, a pair of satin dancing shoes, two other dinner dresses she hadn't been able to resist, and a selection of delicious lingerie lavishly trimmed in French lace.

Dimitrios showed up at the clinic soon after she returned. For an hour or more, they played with Poppy, helping her assemble the brightly colored plastic interlocking building blocks Brianna had found in the toy shop.

After her evening meal, they followed the usual bedtime story ritual. Not until she was asleep for the night did they leave, a heartrending experience that never grew any easier, no matter how often they did it. She was so little, so helpless, so trusting, with no idea of the ordeal awaiting her if the transplant went ahead. And if it didn't, if Brianna turned out not to be a suitable donor…well, that just didn't bear thinking about.

"The day I walk out of this place with Poppy in my arms, we're going to celebrate for a week," Dimitrios vowed, with a last, anguished glance at his daughter's sweet face.

"It's going to happen," Brianna promised, sharing his pain. "And I'll be right there beside you when it does."

He gripped her hand so tightly she winced. "I'm counting on it, sweetheart, more than you can begin to know."

They collected her purchases from the lobby where she'd left them and headed out to the car. "I take it you found what you were looking for," he observed dryly, loading the bags and boxes into the trunk and making an obvious effort to shake off his black mood. "As a matter of interest, did you leave any merchandise for the next customer, or have you bought out the entire shop?"

"I bought what I deemed to be necessary. I'll leave you to decide if I made the right choices."

"Heaven help me, I'm marrying a clothes horse," he moaned.

"Yes, you are," she said cheerfully. "But you knew that when you asked me to be your wife."

That night, he took her for dinner to the Rafina Yacht Club where his fourteen-meter sloop was moored, and the first part of the evening was nothing less than idyllic. They sat at a table by the window and sipped champagne by candlelight. Outside, the moon carved a rippled path over the water and tipped the tall masts of the sailboats with silver.

Brianna wore one of her new outfits, a deep-purple knit cotton dress cut along straight, simple lines. She accessorized it with silver stud earrings, a narrow silver bracelet, her heeled black sandals and a black clutch purse.

Dimitrios, as always, was immaculate in dove-gray Armani trousers, white shirt and navy blazer.

"I'll take you sailing one of these days, when things settle down a bit," he promised. "As they presently stand, though, I'd just as soon be on dry land and able to get to the clinic in a hurry if I need to."

"Yes, of course," she said. "I understand perfectly."

"We'll have a good life, Brianna. You won't regret marrying me."

And that was when the evening fell apart. An older couple, passing by on their way to join a large party at the next table, recognized his voice and stopped. "Dimitrios?" the woman said.

In less time than it took to blink, all the warmth and animation in his face drained away. "Hermione," he returned stiffly, half-rising to his feet in a reluctant show of courtesy. "Mihalis," he added, acknowledging the man with a nod so brief, he might as well not have bothered.

"*Yios.*" The man's eyes, black as coal but with none of its inherent propensity for warmth, skimmed over Brianna. Switching to heavily accented English, he said, "Did I just hear you say you're getting married again?"

"That's right."

"And this is your future wife?"

"Right again."

"So history repeats itself, right down to an exact replica of the original bride. We had heard Cecily's twin was in town and now we know why. Let's hope you don't drive her to an early grave, as well."

Dimitrios grew so forbiddingly still, he might have been turned to stone. The woman, Hermione, however, let out a shocked, "Mihalis!"

Mihalis silenced her with a quelling glare and turned a cheerless smile on Brianna. "Our deepest sympathies, my dear, and all the luck in the world. I'm afraid you're going to need it." Then, overriding his companion's visible distress, he led her away.

Unmoving, Dimitrios watched them leave, his fists clenched at his sides, his eyes stormy, his face the color of old parchment except for two faint strips of color riding his high cheekbones, and his entire body vibrating with rage.

"Dimitrios," Brianna whispered urgently, "who were those people?"

Very slowly he uncurled his fingers, expelled a long breath and resumed his seat. He raised his eyes to hers.

"My parents," he said.

CHAPTER EIGHT

HE'D shocked her, as he'd known he would. Her lovely mouth fell open before she could bring it under control and press it closed again. "Your parents? Dimitrios, you told me they were dead!"

"No," he said. "I told you I have no family but Poppy, and nor do I."

She shook her head. "I don't understand. You just said that man is your father."

"A biological error on his part, I'm sure."

"He spoke as if he hates you!"

"That's because he does."

"But if he's your father! And what about your poor mother…?" Eyes clouded with dismay, she fumbled for her water glass. "I thought she was going to burst into tears."

"But she didn't," he said. "She behaved exactly as she's always behaved around him. Like a downtrodden wife with no right to her own opinions or feelings. I can only suppose she enjoys being molded to the underside of his heel. Eat your fish, Brianna. It's growing cold."

She pushed her plate aside, the grilled red mullet barely touched. "I've just lost my appetite."

"Would you like to order something else? Dessert, perhaps? They make a wonderful almond brandy cake here."

"No. I'd like you to explain what just happened."

"I'd have thought that was self-evident."

"Stop stonewalling, Dimitrios," she snapped, displaying exactly the kind of fire and spirit his mother had never dared fling at his father. "I'm not some stranger poking my nose in where it doesn't belong, I'm the woman you say you want as your wife, and if that's the case, I deserve to know what I'm letting myself in for."

She was right, of course. An explanation wasn't just in order, it was overdue, and better she hear it from him than someone else. "*Endaxi*. Okay." Abandoning his own meal—he'd lost his taste for his grilled octopus, too. His father tended to have that effect on people—he said, "How about coffee and brandy first?"

"Coffee would be nice, but I'll pass on the brandy. You go ahead, though."

He waited until they'd been served, and rolled a mouthful of the very excellent Metaxa Golden Reserve over his palate to erase the lingering aftereffects of his father. "So what would you like to know?"

"Everything," she said promptly.

"Well, you're already aware, of course, that I'm filthy rich."

"Not that it matters to me one way or the other," she said dryly, "but yes, I have noticed."

"So has Mihalis. And that's the problem."

"He didn't look to me as if he's suffering any. The diamond in his pinky ring just about blinded me."

"Ah, but what galls him is that if my tastes also ran to

gaudy, ostentatious jewelry, I could afford a bigger, better, flashier diamond than his."

Again she shook her head. "I'm not following you, Dimitrios. This isn't about jewelry, so why don't you start at the beginning and tell me what's really going on?"

"All right. My father made his first million when he was twenty-one. By the time I was born, eight years later, he'd increased that amount ten times over, and I grew up watching him wield his assets like a weapon to control everyone around him. I saw my mother change from a vivacious, beautiful woman to a passive, listless creature unable to decide what color shoes to wear, without consulting him first. I grew to despise him and pity her, and I'm not sure which I found more distasteful."

"Your mother struck me as a very gentle soul, Dimitrios," Brianna said softly, "and from the little I saw, I think it breaks her heart that she's alienated from you."

"That's her choice."

"Perhaps, but it's a choice no woman should have to make. Is there no possibility of a reconciliation between you?"

"Not as long as my father's alive. He'd never permit it."

"Why not? Surely he must be proud of you? You're smart, successful, respected."

"*Despite* him, not *because* of him, and that's the real problem in a nutshell, Brianna. I learned at a very early age that there are no free lunches with my father. Sooner or later, for every so-called 'favor' he conferred, he'd present me with a bill which was more than I was prepared to pay. So I severed the family ties and struck out on my own."

"I'd have thought that would make him proud of you."

"Wrong, wrong, wrong, *karthula mou!* Certain I couldn't possibly succeed without the almighty Mihalis

Poulos to back me, he waited for me to fail and come crawling back to him."

"Poulos? Where did Giannakis come from?"

"My maternal grandmother. I changed my name when I turned eighteen. Anyhow, when I proved him wrong and succeeded past anything he ever envisioned, he punished me by becoming my biggest, most ferocious business competitor who'd strip me of every euro I own if he could."

"Obviously, he hasn't succeeded."

"Fortunately not. My brain is even more agile than his and I remain one step ahead of him at all times."

"Then you can afford to be generous and drop a vendetta which serves no purpose except to hurt your mother."

"I could." He swirled the brandy in its glass and took another mouthful. "But I won't."

"Why not?"

"Because I'm a proud man, Brianna," he said flatly. "I don't beg, I don't forgive easily, and I never forget."

She regarded him pensively a moment. "What about Poppy? Doesn't she deserve to know her grandparents?"

The old, familiar rage rose up, turning the brandy sour in his stomach. "You just saw the kind of man my father is. Do you really think he gives a rat's ass about my child?"

"He never goes to see her? Never asks about her?"

"Never."

"Your mother, either?"

He let out a bark of laughter as bitter as bile. "Haven't you heard a word I've said, Brianna? My mother daren't even sneeze without his say-so."

"I don't understand any of this." She slumped in her seat, the picture of dejection. "Families are supposed to unite in times of trouble. Look how it brought us together again."

"You have a heart, Brianna. Underneath my reputedly hard-bitten, ruthless tycoon exterior, so do I. I can't say the same for my father."

"Even hard-bitten, ruthless tycoons are supposed to be putty in the hands of their grandchildren."

"In an ideal world, maybe. Not in mine."

She bit her lip. "No wonder you hate him."

"I don't hate him," he was quick to reply. "I refuse to expend the energy it would take. I simply ignore him."

As though to put the lie to his claim, a burst of laughter at his parents' table rolled through the room, and glancing over, he found his father's malevolent gaze fixed on him and Brianna. She noticed it, too, and flinched.

Once upon a time, in his reckless youth, he'd have reacted by hurling himself across the room and smashing his fist into that sneering face. Now he contented himself by trading stare for stare and said evenly, "Don't let him upset you, my darling. He's not worth it. Would you like more coffee, or something a bit stronger to get rid of the bad taste he's left in your mouth?"

She shook her head miserably. "If you don't mind, Dimitrios, I'd really like to get out of here."

"Of course." Reaching for her hand, he brought it to his lips. Across the room, his father watched, his lip curled in amused disdain.

While Dimitrios signed for the meal, Brianna escaped to the ladies' room and sank down on the bench before the mirrored vanity. Her face stared back at her, pale and shocked.

She'd come across her fair share of jealousy and dislike over the years. Professional sabotage, even. In the competitive, unforgiving world of high fashion, success inevitably bred some resentment among those less fortunate. But never had she been the target of the kind of vitriolic loathing Mihalis Poulos had leveled at his only son.

Dimitrios was right, she decided, taking a tube of lip gloss from her purse. The man was toxic and the less they had to do with him, the better.

Just then the door opened and Hermione Poulos slipped into the room. Since they were the only two women present, there was no possible way Brianna could pretend she hadn't seen her. But nor was there any point in lingering and making a tense situation worse, so capping her lip gloss, she dropped it back in her purse and stood up to leave.

Hermione, though, prevented her with an urgent hand on her arm. "*Parakalo,* Despinis Connelly," she practically whimpered, her big brown eyes filled with pleading, "may I have a word?"

Loyalty to Dimitrios told Brianna she should refuse and keep going, but short of pushing the poor woman aside, she had little choice but to stop. "I don't see that we have anything to say to one another, Mrs. Poulos. We certainly have nothing in common."

"We both care deeply about my son, you as the woman who is to become his wife, and I as his mother."

"I'm not sure he believes the latter."

Hermione blinked back the tears welling in her eyes. "He has told you that we are estranged?"

"I more or less figured that out for myself, but yes, he elaborated on the story. We have no secrets from each other."

"Then let me share another one with you that he might not be aware of. A father might qualify his love for his child, but a mother's love is unconditional and eternal. She might not always approve of the things he does or the choices he makes, but she will always hold her child close in her heart."

Not in my experience, Brianna thought.

"Perhaps," Hermione concluded, "one day, my dear, you will discover that for yourself."

Sympathy warring with impatience, Brianna said, "Why are you telling *me* this? Dimitrios is the one you should be talking to."

"I would, if he would listen, but that's not why I asked to speak with you." Her thin, desperate fingers tightened around Brianna's arm. "Tell me, please, how is Poppy? Will she ever be well again?"

"We're hopeful that she will, yes."

"She remains at the Rosegarth?"

"Yes."

"I wish that I could see her."

Impatience winning out over sympathy, Brianna said, "You could, if you chose, Mrs. Poulos. All you have to do is show up. There are no bars on her room. She's in hospital, not prison."

"Mihalis will not permit it."

"Your husband can't stop you, not if you really want to see her, so what you're really saying is that pandering to him matters more to you than giving your sick little granddaughter an hour of your time."

Hermione's mouth trembled and her hand fell away from Brianna's arm. "You make me ashamed," she quavered. "I wish I had your fortitude. But my husband—"

"Is a bully, Mrs. Poulos, and he gets away with it because you let him," Brianna replied bluntly. "Why don't you try standing up to him, for a change? You'd be surprised how much it would boost your confidence, not to mention your self-esteem. Who knows, it might even earn the respect of the son you claim to love so devotedly."

"It isn't easy."

"Not many things worth having ever are. It all boils down to how hard you're willing to fight for them. And now, if you'll excuse me, Dimitrios is waiting to take me home."

"You were in the ladies' room a long time," he remarked, as they headed back along the road to the villa. "I was beginning to think you were being held hostage."

"In a way I was. Your mother cornered me."

He stiffened, his hands suddenly gripping the steering wheel until his knuckles turned white. "I'm surprised my father risked letting her off her leash and out of his sight. What did she want?"

"To know how Poppy is."

"I hope you told her to mind her own business."

"I couldn't do that, Dimitrios. She was so upset and seemed genuinely worried. But I did suggest she could always visit Poppy and see for herself how she's doing."

At that, he hit the brakes with such force that the car nearly skidded off the road. "You did *what?*"

"I told her, if she was all that interested, she should go to the clinic and find out for herself."

"You had no right, Brianna!" he said, his words a whiplash of contained fury. "No right at all to interfere in something that's none of your concern."

"I thought Poppy was my concern," she shot back. "That by volunteering to donate bone marrow, I'd earned the right to make her my concern."

"One thing's got nothing to do with the other. I decide who gets to spend time with my daughter, not you."

"I see." She swallowed painfully, her throat so thick suddenly, it almost choked her.

"No, you don't," he snapped, stepping on the accelerator again and racing the last few hundred yards to the gates of his estate. "You don't have the first idea what's really going on here."

"Why don't you enlighten me, then, Dimitrios? Or does my being a model make me such an airhead that I couldn't possibly understand the intricate workings of your superior mind?"

He slammed on the brakes a second time and killed the engine. In the beat of silence that followed, she heard a gust of frustration escape his lips as he wrestled with his inner demons. Then, his anger at last subsiding, he turned to her in the moonlight and stroked a conciliatory hand down her cheek. "It's complicated, Brianna, okay? Let's just leave it at that. Look, we're home and it's a beautiful night. Don't let what happened at the club spoil things. Let's forget about my parents and take a walk on the beach, and talk about our wedding and the future."

All around them, huge urns of fresh flowers glowed like stars in the moonlight, ready for tomorrow's garden party. A striped tent stood on the far lawn. Chairs swagged in white linen clustered around small tables with floral centerpieces. Stephanotis and gardenias scented the air.

No question but that the setting was perfect. The Garden of Eden recreated to Dimitrios Giannakis's exacting standards, with not a petal out of place, and him its benevolent god, willing to dispense forgiveness for her sins with a touch of his almighty hand!

Bleak with misery and disappointment, she flinched

away from him. Did he really believe a walk on the beach would erase what had just taken place between them?

"What future?" she asked bitterly. "The one in which you issue the orders and I meekly obey them? No thanks, Dimitrios, I'm not that desperate for a husband! You can sneer at your father all you like, but the apple doesn't fall far from the tree, and underneath the charmingly civilized veneer you present to the rest of the world, you're exactly as manipulative and domineering as he is."

He started to reply, but she'd heard enough. Flinging open the door, she climbed out of the car and left him without a backward glance.

Erika met her at the front door. "You're crying, Brianna!" she exclaimed, a rare note of solicitude coloring her words. "Why? What's happened?"

"Ask your boss," she wailed, furious at her own weakness. "He's the one with all the answers."

"Is it Poppy?"

She shook her head and swiped at the accursed tears streaming from her eyes. "No, it's not Poppy."

"A lover's quarrel, then. I could see the pair of you were falling in love." Almost fondly, Erika cradled Brianna's chin in her work-worn hand. "They happen, but the making up is all the sweeter for it. The two of you will work it out, you'll see."

Overwrought, Brianna sobbed, "When did you suddenly decide you were on my side, Erika? I'm trouble, just like my sister, remember?"

"I have second sight," the old woman replied sagely. "I see more than appears on the surface. Dimitrios is right. You look like her, but there the resemblance ends. Dry your tears, *pethi mou,* and I'll make you some *tsai apo votana*—

some herbal tea to soothe your nerves. You're exhausted. Anyone would be in such trying times. You should get some rest. Everything will look quite different after a good night's sleep. Off you go now, before Dimitrios comes in and sees your pretty eyes all red and swollen."

But it would take more than well-meant home remedies to bridge the differences between her and Dimitrios, Brianna knew. Too pent-up to sit passively in her room, she paced the floor like a caged animal and finally, in desperation, flung off her clothes and climbed into her bathing suit.

Except for the distant murmur of voices in the kitchen wing, the house was quiet. Making her way downstairs, she slipped through the French doors leading to the rear terrace, and ran silent as a shadow along the path to the pool deck.

The moon had slipped behind the trees, but underwater lights turned the water into a swath of turquoise satin. Dropping her towel on a chaise, she plunged cleanly into the limpid depths and began a punishing crawl up and down the twenty-meter length.

Her thoughts kept pace with every stroke.

She'd have to move out of his house. First thing tomorrow, she'd pack up her stuff. Find a hotel close to the clinic. Visit Poppy when she knew he wouldn't be there, because she couldn't stand seeing him every day.

What a good thing he'd shown his true colors before it was too late. That he could invite her into his life one minute, then slam the door in her face the next, defied rational explanation.

But that he could speak to her so brutally…be so unfeeling toward the woman who'd given birth to him…!

Oh, he was horrible! She was *so* well rid of him!

In all fairness, though, she had to shoulder some of the

blame. She'd broken every promise she'd made to herself not to get involved with him again. Not to rush blindly into any arrangement that might compromise her hard-won peace of mind and heart.

Yet within a week, she'd agreed to marry him, a man with whom she'd spent little more than thirty days total, and most of those occurring years ago. He was a stranger, someone given to half truths and secrets. What else hadn't he told her? He could be a wife beater, for all she really knew. Be hiding a criminal past behind his exquisitely tailored suits and handmade leather shoes.

She was too willing to be dazzled by illusions of romance. Too easily taken in by appearances. Show her a pair of dark, Mediterranean eyes, a smile that could, when it chose, reduce tempered steel to a molten mass, and the body of a Greek god, and she was lost. A helpless heap of female hormone-driven need.

She shouldn't be allowed to roam free without a keeper.

She was a fool.

He was a liar. He'd deliberately misled her.

And she had finally run out of energy. Her body ached, her lungs were bursting, her pulse racing, and her arms leaden weights she could barely lift. Depleted, she rolled over on her back, closed her eyes, and floated to the ladder hanging over the side of the deep end of the pool. Wearily, she grasped a rung, hauled herself onto the deck and made her way to the chaise where she'd left her towel.

As she bent to pick it up, a tall figure strolled out from the black shadow cast by a nearby palm tree. "Feel better?" Dimitrios inquired coolly.

Not about to admit he'd scared her so badly she almost fell back in the pool, she clutched the towel to her heaving breasts. "As a matter of fact, I do. Not," she couldn't help adding with unvarnished sarcasm, "that it's any of your business."

"When my fiancée disappears from my house without a word to anyone, I make it my business."

"Really?" she drawled with feigned insouciance, and tried to slide past him. "You must have mistaken me for someone who cares."

But he was faster, stronger and more merciless. He lunged forward, lethal as a tiger on its prey, and grabbed her squarely by the shoulders. He was, she realized belatedly, very angry.

"This is not how we settle our differences, Brianna," he informed her. "If I say or do something you don't like, you set me straight. You do *not* cut and run, ever again. Do you understand?"

Incensed, she spat, "Get your hands off me!"

"Make me," he said, his voice deadly, and plastering her wet, scantily-clad body against him, he snagged her dripping hair in one hand, yanked her head back and kissed her, his mouth open, searching. Demanding and taking.

He tasted of rich, mellow Metaxa and frustration. Unbearably erotic and dangerously intoxicating.

Hopelessly enmeshed in craving, she drank him in.

Some distant part of her brain that was still functioning told her she was flirting with disaster, and urged her to extricate herself from a situation fast spiraling out of control. Attempting to heed it, she went to shove him away. But her knees were buckling, a tightness was building between her thighs, and her hands had a mind of their own. They blundered inside his open shirt to rediscover the lovely, sculpted planes of his chest, the lean symmetry of his ribs. His skin was hot and smooth and irresistible.

The more she touched, the more she craved and the farther she strayed past the boundaries of self-preservation. She tested the washboard strength of his midriff—hard, powerful, just like the rest of him. An incorrigible demon of need made her whimper into his mouth.

She heard the sharp intake of his breath and knew she was lost; that in being too daring herself, she'd tacitly invited him to return the favor. His fingers skimmed the length of her torso to search out the sensitive triangle between her thigh and her hip. His thumb strayed inside the leg of her bikini. Circled insolently. Exquisitely. And found its quarry.

Against her will and every shred of common sense at her command, a spasm of tortured pleasure streaked through her. "I hate you," she moaned, her legs falling slackly apart.

"I know," he purred, and touched her again. "I hate you, too."

Rampant desire consumed her. Her entire body contracted in a flood that made an utter mockery of any show of resistance she might have wanted to portray. She was so ready for him, so desperate to feel him skin to skin, heat to heat, that she tore at his shirt like a mad woman.

With a muffled growl, he swept her off her feet and carried her into the palm tree's dense shadow which neither stars nor moon nor man-made light could penetrate. She heard the rustle and rasp of fabric and zipper as he shed his clothes. Modesty and self-preservation lost in the rapacious demands of a hunger at last acknowledged after too long a fast, she kicked off her bikini bottom, tugged loose the strings holding her top in place and flung it aside.

She reached for him, wanting to touch him as he'd

touched her. Intimately, audaciously. She wanted to close her hand around him and hear him groan in an agony of pleasure. She wanted to punish him as he'd punished her and leave his control hanging by a thread, his flesh so tight and yearning for release that he begged for mercy. All this ran through her mind in a molten stream of desire.

But he was not to be so easily subjugated. Closing in on her, hot and naked, he cupped her breasts in his palms and grazed his teeth lightly over her nipples. Teasing and taunting them, with his lips and his tongue until, defeated, she uttered his name on a soft cry, and dissolved in a wash of ecstasy that robbed her of her remaining strength.

He caught her as she collapsed, eased her onto the soft grass and drove into her in one long, hot urgent thrust that sent her over the edge a second time. She clawed at his back. Sank her teeth into the curved muscle of his shoulder. Wrapped her long legs around his waist and clung to him—anything to anchor herself to him as the world tilted on its axis.

He muttered in her ear, Greek and English words jumbled together in graphic exposition of how often he'd imagined this moment, of what she was doing to him. He called her darling and sweetheart, and told her she was the most beautiful woman on earth, and he the luckiest man.

He cursed her for making him come too soon, and within minutes grew hard inside her again and drove them both to new heights of delirium. And when the demons of passion finally were satisfied, she lay tangled with him, a breath of night-cool air teasing her limbs. The storm had passed and taken the anger with it.

The problem, though, still remained, and for all that she tried to dismiss it, it circled restlessly in her mind, tainting the warm afterglow of loving. Easing herself out of his arms, she stood up and went to retrieve her towel and bikini.

He stopped her with a hand around her ankle. "What are you doing?" he inquired lazily.

"Making myself decent again. I can hardly walk into the house stark naked, and nor can you."

"Is our truce so soon ended?"

"What just happened wasn't a truce, Dimitrios."

His fingers drew mesmerizing circles up her calf. "What would you call it then, *agape mou?*"

"A gross error of judgment," she said.

Sensing her disquiet, Dimitrios tightened his grip. "What is it, Brianna? Am I not the lover you thought I was? Did I disappoint you?"

"You know you didn't," she said. "But that doesn't change the fact that what just happened was a huge mistake."

CHAPTER NINE

VERY carefully he removed his hand and propped himself up on one elbow. Her lovely pale shape glimmered in the night, her skin like polished ivory against the dark lush growth of the shrubbery behind her.

"Are you worried I might have left you pregnant?" he asked gently.

"There's that, of course," she said, wrapping herself in her towel as though ashamed to let him see her naked body. "I'm not on the pill, and you didn't use anything."

"I wasn't expecting to make love to you. But, Brianna, what does it matter if you have conceived? A child born of love is cause for celebration, and we'll be married soon enough that no one need know we didn't wait until our wedding night to pledge ourselves to each other."

"A hasty marriage isn't the solution to everything."

"There's another problem I don't know about?"

"There is, and you know very well what it is."

No sweeping stuff under the rug with her, he thought wryly. She wouldn't let him get away with a damned thing. "You're still angry with me."

"My anger isn't the issue. It's yours that worries me. Deny it all you like, but this business with your parents is eating you alive. Put an end to it, Dimitrios, please. I've had enough in-fighting with my own family to last me a lifetime. Don't ask me to take on yours, as well."

If ruining the moment was her intention, she was succeeding admirably. All traces of passion as dead as last year's roses, he pulled on his pants and drew up the zipper. "And exactly how do you propose I go about doing that?"

"Swallow your pride and talk to your father. Declare a truce. If you could do that with me, you can do it with him."

"It'll be cold day in hell before I grovel to Mihalis Poulos, my dear."

"Come on, Dimitrios, be the bigger man," she persisted. "You need your family at this time. Poppy needs her grandparents."

"She has you and me and everyone else in my house. We are all the family she needs."

"What if your parents need her?"

"They do not. My father refuses to acknowledge her, and my mother—"

"Would defy him, if she knew she had your support. Instead you go through her to try to punish him and it's not working, Dimitrios, because he doesn't care. The only one hurting here is the person least able to arm herself against you."

"Leave it, Brianna," he said harshly. "Don't push me on this. My mind is made up."

Her sigh gusted into the night, rife with frustration. "Is this the example you want to set for Poppy, Dimitrios? To hold on to a grudge at any price?"

"If it's justified, yes."

"Even if she turns on you one day? You're human, after all. You make mistakes, just like the rest of us. What if you do something she decides she can't forgive? How will you live with yourself?"

"It won't happen. I won't allow it."

"You won't *allow*…?" She lapsed into a silence that hung in the air, an implicit threat. Then she spoke again. "What if I can't live with a man who thinks he's God?"

He didn't like what he heard in her voice. "Are you saying we're at an impasse, Brianna? That this is a deal breaker and if I don't give way on it, you won't marry me?"

"Yes," she said. "That's exactly what I'm saying."

"I don't deal well with ultimatums."

"Of course you do," she shot back scornfully. "As long as you're the one issuing them. And if, in the process, you trample all over a few hearts, well that's just the price of doing business, isn't it?"

"Whose heart am I trampling? Yours?"

"Sorry to disappoint you, but no. Mine is made of sterner stuff. I've lost you once and lived to tell about it. I can do it again, if I have to. Your mother, though, she's a different story. Between the pair of you, you and your father are going to end up putting her in her grave."

"So let me get this straight. Either I agree to your terms or you walk. May I ask where Poppy fits in the picture?"

"Exactly where she deserves to be—as my top priority. She isn't the problem here, Dimitrios. You are. In your own way, you're as dysfunctional a parent as Cecily was, and our mother before that."

No one else would have dared speak to him so bluntly, laying bare truths he didn't want to acknowledge. But she was different. She always had been. Beneath that delicate exterior lay a tempered-steel core of integrity that refused to be compromised. How could he not respect that?

He wiped a hand down his face. "You do realize this is emotional blackmail, pure and simple?"

"Of course," she returned blithely. "Surprising though you might find it, my IQ does register on the positive side of zero, which leaves me well able to put two and two together and come up with four."

Choking back a laugh, he said, "Okay, I'll make you a deal. Marry me, and I'll agree to try to sort things out with my mother—my *mother,* Brianna, not my father."

"When?"

"Is tomorrow soon enough?"

She edged away from the palm tree and onto the pool deck, her face a study in suspicion. "It's not like you to capitulate without a fight. Where's the catch?"

"There isn't one," he said, and following her, caught her around the waist. "I want you more than I don't want the alternative, that's all." And pulling her back into the shadows, he kissed her again.

At first she resisted him, holding herself stiff as a board.

"Be patient with me, *agape mou,*" he whispered against her closed lips. "Remember, I'm a work in progress."

She made a soft, helpless sound in her throat and wound her arms around his neck. Her mouth bloomed under his, hot and sweet.

His body quickened in a burst of need that staggered him. Bracing himself against the tree, he tossed aside her towel and yanked down his fly. In one swift move, he lifted her so that she straddled him, and slid to the hilt in her sleek and eager flesh.

She convulsed around him almost immediately; spasm after mind-numbing spasm that pushed him beyond anything mortal man could hope to withstand. Desperate to prolong the pleasure, to distract himself from the siren song that was her body, he doggedly recited to himself the months of the year. *Ianouarios…Fevrouarios…Martios*….

April made a fool of him. He came in a blinding rush, spilling into her endlessly, violently, until he had nothing left to give. Drained, and still buried inside her, he sagged at the knees and lowered them both to the grass, too depleted to support his own weight, let alone hers. "If you don't end up pregnant after that," he panted, when at last he was able to speak again, "then one or both of us needs to see a fertility specialist."

Her breast rose in a sigh. "I didn't mean to play Russian roulette again. You caught me off guard."

"I caught me, as well." He wrapped her more securely against him. "Not surprising, really. I'm making up for four years of lost time."

"It wasn't all bad. At least you ended up with Poppy."

He'd feared all along that sooner or later he'd have to share everything with her; that she deserved better than the laundered truth he'd so far given her. If golden opportunity was what he'd been waiting for, the one she'd just handed him couldn't be beaten. "And I wouldn't be without her," he began. "Until you came back, she was my whole life, but—"

She stopped him dead with an ear-splitting shriek as a jet of cold water sluiced over them. Too late, he realized that the in-ground sprinkler system had been turned off only where the tables and tent were set up. The rest of the grounds were receiving their nightly soaking.

Cursing, he rolled to his feet and took her with him. Another blast caught them in the crossfire, streaking over his pants and spraying the length of her spine. Grabbing her towel, he thrust it at her and shoved her toward the pool deck, then raced back to collect their remaining clothes. He didn't fancy having one of tomorrow's guests stumbling over her bikini or his boxers.

Joining her, he said, "Not exactly how I'd hoped to end the evening, but now you know how I keep my gardens so green and lush."

Drops of water spiked her eyelashes and clung to the ends of her hair like so many scattered diamonds. Her teeth were chattering, likely as much from shock as cold, and she looked thoroughly offended. "I thought someone had turned a hose on us."

"It'd take more than that to put out the fire between us, *agape mou!*" he laughed. "Come on, I'll sneak you in by the side door and up the back stairs. With any luck, you'll make it to your room without bumping into anyone."

"I can only hope," she said tartly. "I've had about as many surprises as I can handle for one night."

Close to an international crowd of a hundred showed up the next afternoon, among them several personnel Brianna had met at the hospital over the past two weeks. The vast majority of guests, though, were strangers, and although some did a double take, most managed to mask their surprise when Dimitrios introduced her as Poppy's aunt and his future bride.

"How very lovely to meet you," they murmured politely, giving her a discreet once-over.

And "What a refreshing return to normality for little Poppy, to have two parents again."

They didn't add, "Especially when one's a dead ringer for her late mother," but Brianna was sure that must be what they were thinking. Once out of earshot, they gathered in little cliques and exchanged knowing glances over their champagne flutes and teacups.

"I imagine you're finding this a bit of a baptism by fire," Noelle remarked sympathetically at one point. Petite, blond and elegant in lavender shantung, she looked more like a ballet dancer than the head of a prestigious transplant team, and was a perfect foil for Dimitrios's dark good looks. "Don't let it get you down, Brianna. Just be yourself and enjoy the afternoon."

Easier said than done, though. She and Dimitrios made a handsome pair and Brianna felt very much the third wheel, tagging along in their wake as they mingled with the crowd. Still, she made the effort, smiling and nodding in all the right places, but the strain must have shown because after a while, Dimitrios took pity on her and sent her off to the refreshment tent for a reviving cup of tea.

Not a good idea, as it turned out. Only a few people clustered around the linen-draped buffet table, among them four women, all Americans, were helping themselves to an array of tiny pastries and deep in conversation not meant for anyone else's ears, least of all hers.

"Marrying the identical-twin aunt takes keeping it all in the family a bit too far, if you ask me," one in robin's-egg-blue brocade declared.

"Not the smartest choice he could have made, I agree," another put in. "If she's anything like Cecily, he's in for a load of trouble he doesn't need, what with his daughter being so ill and all. Noelle's a much better candidate."

The third nodded conspiratorially. "Grist for the gossip mills, though. The buzz around Athens is he met both sisters at some sort of celebrity yachting party years ago, and this is the one he was really after, but Cecily put the moves on him and trapped him into marrying her instead."

"Just goes to show even Dimitrios Giannakis makes a mistake once in a while. Kind of gives hope to the rest of us mere mortals, doesn't it?"

"That's harsh," the remaining member of the quartet said. "If the rumors are true and this is a love match that's been forced onto the back burner all this time, I say good luck to them."

"And they'll need it. Sixty-seven percent of second marriages end in divorce, and I'd lay money on theirs being one of them," robin's-egg-blue brocade pronounced sanctimoniously.

Resisting an uncharitable urge to stuff the entire tray of pastries down the woman's throat, Brianna took aim and fired a shot of her own. "If saving face is at all important to you, you might want to keep that opinion to yourself," she said sweetly, her hand admirably steady as she accepted a cup of Earl Grey from the uniformed maid manning the sterling tea service. "Dimitrios and I, you see, plan to be one of the remaining twenty-three percent."

The collective gasp that followed indicated she'd scored a direct hit. It should have made her feel better, but it didn't. Rather, it underscored what she'd believed from the outset. She and Dimitrios were getting too far ahead of themselves.

Just that morning, on the way back from visiting Poppy, she'd tried talking him out of going public so soon with news of their engagement, if such it could be called. "It's not the time," she'd argued. "This afternoon's about honoring the people on your guest list. It's nor fair to steal their thunder."

He'd disagreed. "Face it, Brianna, when it comes to news like this, there's no such thing as the right time. It's going to cause a stir, no matter when we announce it. We might as well get it over and done with."

"But I'm not ready to broadcast it to the whole world."

"Why not? Are you still having second thoughts about us?"

"No," she said slowly. "It's more that I'm still getting used to the idea of us being a couple, and I don't want to share it with anyone else just yet."

"That's all very fine, sweetheart," he reminded her, "but you forget my father already knows. This is happy news, Brianna, the best, and I'm not about to stand back and let him taint it with his own particular brand of poisonous cynicism."

Against her better judgment, she'd allowed herself to be persuaded. But what she'd just overheard warned her that Mihalis Poulos didn't have a monopoly on poison. And once again Carter's advice came back to haunt her. *Take care, Brianna....*

We're rushing into this too fast, she thought miserably. *Too much is going on, and we're losing sight of the most important person here, who is Poppy. The minute this party's over, I'm going to talk to Dimitrios. I have to convince him to slow down.*

Her plan hit a snag when, with the sun casting long shadows over the garden, a white limousine purred up the drive and drew to a stop not far from where she and Dimitrios stood waving goodbye to the last of the departing guests. Noelle had been called back to the hospital just after five o'clock. Now it was almost seven, and well past the time for latecomers to show up.

Disappointed, because she desperately wanted to be alone with him and set a few things straight, Brianna said, "Are you expecting someone, Dimitrios?"

"*Neh.* I have a surprise for you. We'll be three for dinner tonight. Hermione is joining us."

"Your *mother?*"

"That's right. I called her this morning." He linked his fingers in hers. His eyes caressed her. His smile bathed her in warmth. "You see, *calli mou,* I do listen when you speak. I do try to please you every way I know how."

He was doing it again. Ambushing her with his compassion; disarming her when she was in battle mode. He was worse than a chameleon, she thought helplessly. One part of him was all about power and success and pride and ambition; the other, a testament to the generosity and kindness he shared only with a few select individuals, including her. How was she supposed to combat that?

"Well?" he said, nudging her gently. "Do we invite her in, or do I send her away again?"

She swung her gaze to the woman hovering beside the open door of the car, as though uncertain of her welcome. Brianna could only imagine the courage it had taken for her to get this far. "We ask her in, of course. And Dimitrios? Thank you."

"Efharisto," Hermione murmured in an aside to Brianna, as Dimitrios attended to predinner drinks. "I know I am here only because of your intercession with my son."

They sat on the west-facing verandah in comfortable wicker armchairs, with a tray of *mezedes* on the table in front of them, the olives, chunks of ripe red tomatoes drizzled in oil, slivers of octopus in wine, tzatziki and deep-fried calamari a meal in themselves.

Candles flickered in brass hurricane lamps strung among the vines overheard and nested at the base of the potted hibiscus shrubs fringing the perimeter of the terra-cotta-tiled floor. Hidden somewhere out of sight in the garden, a lemon tree in bloom perfumed the air. Below the verandah, the lawns dropped down in a series of manicured terraces to the shore. The sun sat low on the horizon, its dying rays staining the sky pink and orange and mauve.

An idyllic setting for a family reunion long overdue, some might have thought, but it was spoiled by the nervous tension simmering in the atmosphere. Hermione's fingers lay knotted in her lap. Her foot in its expensive suede pump tapped an anxious tattoo on the terra-cotta tiles. Her eyes flitted from Dimitrios to the glass doors opening into the house, as though she was unsure whether she should stay and face whatever the evening brought, or leave now, while she still had the chance.

Brianna felt terribly sorry for her. "I'm glad he asked you here, and so glad you came, Hermione. I'm sure it wasn't easy for you to accept his invitation."

"Mihalis doesn't know I'm here," she said, with another furtive glance around. "He thinks I'm visiting a friend."

It was on the tip of Brianna's tongue to say she was surprised the poor woman was allowed to have friends. Luckily, Dimitrios returned to the table just then and spared her having to think of a more suitable reply.

"An occasion such as this calls for a special toast," he announced, plucking a bottle of Krug from a silver ice bucket and pouring into three spun-glass flutes. "*Kherete,*

Mother. Welcome. I can't recall the last time you and I sat down together and enjoyed a glass of wine."

"I can," she said. "It was the day you came home with an honors degree from the London School of Economics. I was so proud of you. I still am, Dimitrios. I always will be. Not that it matters to you one way or the other, I suppose."

He cleared his throat and studied the bubbles rising in his glass as if they were the most fascinating things he'd ever come across. "It matters, Mother, and I'm proud of you, too. I know it wasn't easy for you to come here tonight. I can't imagine Mihalis was any too pleased when he heard."

"Well, he hasn't heard, at least not yet, although I suppose I can't keep it from him indefinitely. But whatever the price I have to pay, it won't compare to what it's cost me to be alienated from my son and grandchild. So, if you don't mind, I'd like to propose a toast, as well." Eyes shining with suppressed tears, she raised her glass. "To the future. May it bring you both all the happiness you deserve. And to my dear granddaughter, that she may soon be well again and back home where she belongs."

Regaining his composure, he clinked the rim of his flute against hers. "Better yet, how about, to all four of us?"

I'm going to cry, Brianna thought, barely able to swallow her wine.

Across the table Dimitrios caught her eye. "And most especially to my beautiful fiancée, for her wisdom and patience. I'm a better man because of you, Brianna, *calli mou.*"

Dear heaven, what a talent he had for laying claim to her heart! What an abundance of charm! He knew exactly the right buttons to push to make her cast aside her doubts and think only of how lucky they were to have found each other again.

Hermione beamed through her tears. "So when is the marriage to take place?"

"As soon as possible. Yesterday, if it was up to me," Dimitrios said. "I lost this beautiful woman once already. I won't risk losing her again."

"I can see that you love her very much."

Reaching for Brianna's hand, he brushed his mouth over her knuckles. "She is my life," he declared, piercing her with a glance of such unbridled hunger that she blushed. "Even now, with things about as grim as they can get with Poppy, Brianna gives me hope of better times to come. With her by my side, I can face whatever the future holds."

"Which is exactly as it should be." Hermione blinked away a fresh onslaught of happy tears. "If you'll let me, I'd love to help with the wedding—unless your parents, Brianna…?"

"My father died when I was a baby, and my mother when I was nineteen," she said. "As for a wedding, I really haven't given it much thought. It doesn't seem terribly important in the greater scheme of things."

"Because of Poppy," Hermione said gently. "I understand. But, *pethi mou,* your wedding day is important, too. You should be able to look back on it with pleasure for the happy memories it holds, not regret that it passed by without your noticing."

"Let's not forget whose wedding this is, Hermione," Dimitrios warned, all the old reserve back in his voice. "It's up to Brianna to decide what she wants."

"Well, yes…I didn't mean to push my way in where I don't belong."

She shrank back in her chair, looking so crestfallen that Brianna rushed to reassure her. "As mother of the groom, of course you belong, Hermione. And once we set a date, I'll be glad of your input."

Erika came to remove the appetizers just then, and a short time later brought in the main course. Conversation resumed on a more general note after that, easing the tension and lending an almost festive air to the occasion. But it all came to an abrupt end when a fracas at the front door heralded the uninvited and decidedly unwelcome arrival of a fourth member to the party.

Recognizing her husband's raised voice, Hermione turned ashen and froze with her fork halfway to her mouth. As for Dimitrios... Brianna cringed at the murderous expression on his face. Iron-jawed, he rose from the table, his eyes blazing, his fists clenched.

A moment later Mihalis Poulos erupted onto the scene, with Alexio trailing behind in a fruitless attempt to stop him. Ignoring him, Mihalis adjusted his heavy gold cuff links and tugged the lapels of his cream linen jacket in place. "What happened, son?" he drawled. "Did my invitation get lost in the mail?"

Dimitrios impaled him in a feral, unblinking stare. "Brianna," he said softly, "please take my mother inside and wait there for me."

She hesitated, torn about how she should respond. Instinct told her to throw herself between him and his father; to stop the inevitable and violent confrontation she knew was coming. Years of bitterness and resentment had finally come to a head. Tonight it would end, and only one man would emerge the winner.

She had little doubt who that would be. Mihalis was big,

but Dimitrios was bigger. Stronger. Younger by almost thirty years.

"Brianna," he said again.

"No." She edged around the table to grasp his arm. "Dimitrios, don't play into his hands. Don't let him goad you into doing something you'll regret."

He shook her off as easily, as casually as if she were a fly. "*Now,* Brianna. This is between Mihalis and me. We don't need an audience."

"You might need a lawyer, though. Hurt him badly enough, and you could wind up spending the next twenty-five years behind bars. How much use will you be as a father, then?"

Just briefly she thought she'd reached him. She felt, rather than heard his indrawn breath. Sensed rather than saw the sudden doubt assailing him.

But Mihalis hadn't missed a thing. "Now, there's the difference between you and me, *yios,*" he sneered. "I've never felt the need to hide behind a woman's skirts. No wonder your first wife ran around on you. She probably grew tired of having to fight your battles."

At that, Dimitrios let out a roar and lunged. The table flew over, smashing dishes and spreading a mess of orzo and olive-stuffed breast of pheasant everywhere. Shards of crystal glittered on the terra-cotta tiles.

Alexio yelped and ran back inside the house. And because she was too late to stop the carnage, Brianna did as she'd been asked in the first place and hurried Hermione away from the scene.

Erika met them in the hall. "Take her to the sitting room, Brianna," she ordered calmly. "This is not something either of you need to see."

"Is Alexio calling the police?"

Erika laughed grimly. "If you think Dimitrios can't deal with that man by himself, *pethi mou,* you still have much to learn about him."

Outside, something else fell with a crash. Wincing, Brianna said, "How about an ambulance, then? At this rate, they're both going to need one."

"Go." Erika ushered them firmly toward the big, formal sitting room, as serenely elegant with its ivory walls and silk-upholstered sofas as the terrace currently was in a shambles. "You don't care for brandy, I know, but I will bring you coffee, which you will sit and enjoy until Dimitrios joins you."

"This is my fault," Hermione whispered, shaking so badly Brianna was afraid she might collapse.

"No, *Kyria,* this is not about you," Erika declared. "This is between your husband and your son. It's been a long time coming and there's nothing you or the police or anyone else can do but let them settle their differences, once and for all."

She paused and tilted her head, listening. "And it would seem," she finished, "that they have done just that. I'll bring coffee for three, and a decanter of Morello cherry liqueur. Dimitrios enjoys it once in a while, as a change from Metaxa."

Brianna realized then that silence reigned outside, and the only sound was the inner thudding of her heart.

CHAPTER TEN

HE BRUSHED one hand against the other. It was done.

He should have felt vindicated. Purged. He didn't.

Grimacing, he turned back to the house. To the villa he'd built as a monument to his success. Twilight dusted its walls. Lights streamed from the windows, warm and yellow. But he felt only the coldness of another in a long list of empty victories. At the end of the day, what did any of them matter compared to a home, a wife, a healthy child. A family living in harmony and bound together by love. Ordinary, everyday pleasures which most people took for granted, but which he had never known.

The front door opened and the woman who'd been both mother, mentor and servant to him for the last nine years stepped out. "Coffee's waiting," she said, as if nothing untoward had occurred.

When he didn't reply, she came down the steps to stand next to him. "No point in brooding, Dimitrios. You did what had to be done. He left you with no choice. Now it's over."

"Yes," he said, but he'd seen the horror in Brianna's eyes before she took his mother away, and knew it wasn't quite over, not yet. "Where are they?"

"Waiting for you in the sitting room."

He nodded and touched her shoulder. "I'm glad you're on my side, Erika."

She slapped at his hand with rough affection. "Which other side is there, dolt? Get inside and speak with your women."

He found Brianna standing at the window, her fingers drumming lightly on the sill, her face unreadable. His mother huddled in the corner of one of the two settees facing each other in front of the fireplace, and she...

She was only fifty-eight, but underneath the expensive clothes, the stylish hairdo, and all that estheticians and cosmetics could do to preserve the illusion of youth, she looked old, beaten down, afraid, and he felt a pang of guilt that he'd stood by and done nothing to help her until now.

"He's gone and he won't be back, Mother," he told her, advancing into the room.

She regarded him anxiously. "Is he all right?"

"He didn't leave with a smile on his face, if that's what you're asking."

"I must go to him."

"No, you must not. You must stay here."

"Overnight, you mean?"

"For as many nights as it takes him to come to his senses." He helped himself to one of the demitasses on the library table and drained it in one gulp. Erika had made *metrios,* medium-sweet coffee, and for once he was glad of the sugar. He needed something to chase away the sour taste in his mouth.

"Dimitrios is right," Brianna said, coming forward. "At least here you'll be safe."

"Safe?" Hermione stared at them as though they were

both certifiably insane. "Mihalis would never hit *me*. He's never lifted a hand against me in his life."

"Abuse doesn't have to be a physical thing, Mother," Dimitrios said wearily. "There are other, more subtle ways to wear a person down."

She raised a few more feeble objections—she'd be putting them out, his father would be worried, she had no change of clothes, no makeup, not even a toothbrush. But in the end he overcame her objections and she allowed Erika to take her upstairs.

"Well," he said, as the door closed behind them and left him alone with Brianna, "no broken bones or blood, as you can see."

"Your shirt's torn," she said frostily.

He shrugged. "Shirts can be replaced."

"And husbands, fathers?" Her light-blue eyes bored into him, laser beams of disgust. "Are they disposable items, too?"

"I didn't kill or maim him, if that's what's worrying you, Brianna. I kicked him out. Sent him packing with his tail between his legs. His pride's badly dented, he's a little dusty, and his suit won't be fit to wear again, but he's in one piece otherwise."

"I see. And do you settle all your differences with your fists?"

"What the hell would you have had me do?" he inquired irascibly. "Stand idly by and let him terrorize my mother? Insult you—*again?*"

"Of course not. But couldn't you have reasoned with him? Did you have to be so violent?"

"Yes," he said. "I did. Because reason is only effective if the other party's willing to listen. And my father hears only his own voice. And because there comes a time when a man has to take a stand. For me, that time came tonight. He invaded my home. He threatened my household staff. He intimidated you and my mother. He behaved like a thug. Don't ask me to reason with a man like that."

"You could have called the police."

"And give him the satisfaction of thinking I couldn't deal with him myself?" Frustrated, he shook his head and, lifting the decanter of cherry liqueur parked on the tray next to the coffee cups, poured himself a hefty measure. "No, Brianna, this was between him and me, no one else."

"What if he charges you with assault?"

"His pride won't let him."

"Like father, like son," she muttered, her lovely mouth set in obstinate disapproval.

He downed his drink and poured another. He was tired and spattered with food. His body felt as if it had gone ten rounds with a sumo wrestler. His right hand was bruised, the knuckles scraped raw. "I don't have to defend myself to you, Brianna."

"No, you don't," she agreed loftily. "You can get drunk, instead. Excuse me for not wanting to stand here and watch."

She went to stalk past him, but he caught her and swung her round to face him, his fingers spanning her slender wrist in an iron grip. "Don't you dare walk out on me again."

She glared at him, outraged. "Don't you dare manhandle *me. Ever!*"

Aghast, ashamed, he released her and raised both hands in surrender. "Forgive me. I'm not at my best right now. Believe it or not, I don't make a habit of brawling."

She sighed and lowered her gaze. "I know that."

"Do you?"

"Yes," she said. "You were in an impossible situation. Most men would probably have reacted as you did."

"The point is, I'm not most men. I'm his son. That he's finally been called to account for his actions is something only I could accomplish. It's the old law of the jungle, Brianna. A case of the aging lion accepting someone younger and more powerful has taken over as king."

"You really believe he understands that?"

Dimitrios thought of the last look his father had turned on him, before he crawled into his car and was driven away. He'd seen a lurking respect in those black, indomitable eyes; a certain sick satisfaction, even, as though he'd finally proved to himself and the rest of the world that the man he professed to hate was worthy of being called his son. "Yes, I do. For all his faults, Mihalis is no fool. He knows when he's beaten."

"How do you suppose he found out where your mother was?"

"Most likely from the chauffeur who drove him here. He was the same man who brought my mother, and was waiting in the same car to take her and my father home again. His staff are as much under his thumb as she is."

"You never did explain how you persuaded her to break rank and visit you."

"I told her if she really wanted to reestablish a connection with me and my family, my door was open. She asked when would be a good time to stop by, I invited her to dinner tonight, and she came."

"Simple as that?"

He didn't tell her Hermione had burst into tears when

she heard his voice, or that it wasn't until then that he realized how much he loved her despite everything. That was something he himself had yet to digest. "Not quite. I was as surprised as you when she actually showed up. I thought she'd lose her nerve at the last minute."

"She must have known your father would find out, sooner or later."

"That was a risk she chose to take. I didn't browbeat her into it, and I didn't beg. That's not my style."

She chewed her lips thoughtfully. "So, what are you going to do about her now? She won't stay here, if that's what you're hoping. She believes her place is with her husband, no matter how he treats her. He's what she's used to. She'd be lost without him."

"I agree. But the dust needs to settle first." He raked his fingers through his hair and dislodged a sliver of olive. "Look, can we table this discussion until tomorrow? I need a shower in the worst way."

She let out an exclamation and peered at his damaged hand. "You need a first-aid kit more! If there was no blood involved in your little fracas with your father, what do you call this?"

"It's nothing. A scratch, that's all. We scuffled, and I…connected with the verandah wall by mistake."

"Right!" She rolled her eyes scornfully. "Go take your shower, for pity's sake. You're bleeding all over the rug."

"Will I see you later? We've had hardly any alone time today. I haven't even told you how lovely you look."

"You were so busy being the attentive host, I didn't think you'd noticed."

"How could I not have noticed, when you left every other woman in the shade?" He let his gaze drift over her in leisurely appreciation, amazed as always by her match-less elegance and beauty. "The dress, the hat, the shoes...." He made a circle of his forefinger and thumb. "Perfection!"

"I'm not wearing the hat now."

"I noticed. And if I have my way, you soon won't be wearing the dress or shoes, either."

"Forget it," she said, rolling her lovely eyes. "You've had enough excitement for one day."

But half an hour later, just as he'd finished shaving and went to leave his bathroom, he heard the quiet click of his bedroom door opening. Hastily slinging a towel around his hips, he went to investigate and by the light of a reading lamp next to the bed, caught Brianna tiptoeing toward the nightstand. She'd changed into a flame-colored robe cinched tightly at the waist, and loosened her hair so that it floated in a dark cloud around her shoulders, and her feet were bare.

"Ahem," he murmured.

The very picture of wide-eyed guilt, she spun around. "Oh," she said, and gulped when she saw his state of undress. "I did knock, but when you didn't answer, I thought you might still be in the shower."

"No. I'm done."

"Yes...well..." She averted her gaze. "I brought you this. I thought you might need it. Your hand looked...pretty badly swollen."

She thrust an ice pack at him, tugged the tie belt at her waist a little tighter and actually blushed when she saw his smile. He was tempted to tell her his hand wasn't the only thing swelling up. Points south of his waist weren't exactly hibernating, either. But she was so clearly agitated, he didn't have the heart to tease her.

She was shy, he realized, charmed. Uncertain of her welcome. This beautiful, spirited creature, the envy of women the world over and surely desired by any man who didn't have both feet in the grave, wasn't nearly as self-assured as she'd like him to think.

"Efharisto," he said gravely. "That was kind of you."

"You're welcome." She shifted from one foot to the other and cast a longing glance at the door. "Well then, I'll be going."

"Please don't," he said, and ghosting a hand down her spine, drew her to him and touched his mouth to hers.

She wilted against him like a flower left too long without water, and let out a sigh. "I shouldn't be here."

"Why not?"

"Your mother's asleep in a room just down the hall."

"If we're very quiet, we probably won't wake her."

"Oh, it's not that, Dimitrios, and you know it."

"What is it, then, *calli mou?*"

"I'm here because I couldn't stay away," she admitted forlornly, "even though I keep telling myself that jumping into bed together won't resolve the problems we face. I'm the one who insisted last night was a mistake, yet here I am, ready to repeat it. It's wrong. We need to get to know each other properly all over again, and only then…"

"Hush," he said, and kissed her a second time, dipping his tongue fleetingly into her sweet mouth. "This *is* getting to know each other properly all over again."

"I'd really like to believe that."

"What's stopping you, Brianna? What is it about me, about us, that you don't trust? Is it that I've asked you to marry me, but haven't yet put a ring on your finger?"

"No!"

"Because I intend to remedy that this week. I'd have done it sooner, but I've had a few things on my mind."

"I don't care about a ring!"

"Are you afraid I'll turn into my father and browbeat you into wifely submission?"

She almost smiled. "That's the least of my worries."

He drew his fingertip in a straight line from her throat to her cleavage, past her rib cage and over the firm, smooth curve of her belly to the juncture of her thighs. "Do I not stir you to ungovernable passion?"

Her eyes grew heavy with desire. Her breathing quickened and a shudder ran through her. "You make me crazy," she whispered.

He loosened the knot at her waist and parted the folds of her robe. Underneath, she wore a whisper of a bra and tiny panties; two nonsense strips of peach-tinted satin trimmed with lace that concealed nothing. Her nipples pushed hard as pebbles against the bra; her panties were warmly damp against his palm.

"How crazy?" he muttered at her ear.

She responded by stepping back a pace, stripping away his towel and running her hands down his flanks to cradle him.

He was already hard. Had been from the moment he'd discovered her in his room. And she seemed fascinated by his arousal, displaying a curiosity at once naive and bold. "You are so beautiful and strong and perfect," she breathed.

Her touch, delicate as butterflies, lethal as fire, almost finished him off before he'd begun, and he couldn't allow that. Swinging her into his arms, he carried her to the bed and lowered her to the mattress. He ached to feel her clench around him, to fuse his body with hers and find again the release only she could bring, but the satisfaction, though exquisite, would be all too brief, and it had been such a long, long time since they'd made love at leisure.

"First, we get rid of these," he said, making short work of the bra and panties.

She lay naked before him in the lamplight, and for the first time since she'd come back into his life, he was able to look his fill at her naked body. She was as beautiful as ever, her breasts still small and firm, the nipples tinted the same dusty rose he remembered from before, her hips flaring in a graceful, narrow curve, her waist so tiny he could span it with his hands.

The difference was there'd been no hesitation back then, no doubt. She'd reveled in his scrutiny, offering him all that she was, her hunger as urgent and all-consuming as his, her flesh pliant and willing. This time, caution warred with desire and she lay frozen beneath his gaze, her arms pinned at her sides, her thighs clamped together.

Patiently, persistently, he kissed every exposed inch of her: the slope of her breasts, the inner curve of her elbow, the arch of her instep, the back of her knees. And inch by inch, she melted under his ministrations. Most of her, at least, until, capturing her gaze, he said softly, "Open your legs, Brianna."

She blinked and swallowed, her mind clearly rebelling at the idea, but her body had a will of its own and when he blew a damp breath against the top of her thighs, they fell apart and gave him leave to do what he'd never done to her before. He put his mouth against her and seduced her with his tongue, sliding it between the satin folds of her flesh to search out the hidden nub at her center.

Her skin had the texture of gossamer, the sheen of a

pearl, and she tasted of honey and woman and passion on the verge of explosion. He delved deep with his tongue, once, twice, three times, and felt the tremors racing through her. Heard her shocked gasp fade into a long, low moan as she shattered, her body arching off the bed in mindless torment, her fists clutching at his hair.

He soothed her, stroking her, kissing her, and when she subsided into dreamy acquiescence, he seduced her again. And again, she climaxed, faster, harder this time. She clawed at his shoulders, trying to drag his body up to cover hers, to accept him between her legs, and all the while begging amid fractured sobs, "Please, Dimitrios…all of you…now, please…!"

"I have nothing here…no *profilaktiko,*" he said hoarsely, remembering too late that he never kept any in the house because if he was going to spend the night with a woman, she wasn't the kind he'd bring home to meet his daughter.

"I don't care!" Brianna cried, guiding him deep into the hot, wet temple of her body. "I *want* to have your baby!"

She didn't really mean it. Just yesterday, she'd worried she might get pregnant. So he'd be careful. He'd give her the satisfaction she craved, pleasure himself as much as he dared, then pull out at the last minute.

Just as it took two to come together in complete intimacy, though, so it took two to agree when the time was right to break apart. And she was of a different mind, one that rendered him blind to everything but the driving need to possess her. Fully and completely and forever.

"Thee mou!" he ground out, his lungs burning and the sweat beading his brow as she climaxed a third time. He was lost, a leaf caught in a raging river, helpless to direct

his own fate. Accepting defeat, he poured into her, gave her everything he had, everything he was. She'd stolen his heart years ago. She might as well have the rest of him.

When he could breathe again, he stroked a damp strand of hair from her face and said, "Someday we're going to take this slowly and make it last all night. Just don't ask me when. It could take years before I'm able to pace myself."

She smiled and closed her eyes. "May I ask you something else instead?"

"Anything, *calli mou.*"

"Are you going to kick me out of your bed now and send me back to my own room?"

"Not a chance. You belong here, with me."

"Oh, good," she said, and turning on her side, curled up against him and fell asleep.

He was gone when she awoke the next morning, but a glass of chilled orange juice stood on the bedside table, and a single perfect red rose lay next to her on his pillow, proof positive, if proof she needed, that last night hadn't been a dream.

She brushed the velvety petals against her cheek and inhaled their delicate fragrance. She couldn't recall the last time she'd slept so soundly or awoken filled with such joy.

Yesterday's petty anxieties seemed woefully unimportant in the light of the new day. Dimitrios was right. It was time to banish her insecurities. Time to let go all the black and bitter memories eating away at her. The sting of Cecily's betrayal, the pain of her death, were in the past, but Brianna and Dimitrios, they were the present and the future. Life wasn't perfect—that would only be the case when Poppy was well again—but it was good. It was filled with hope again.

Throwing back the covers, she put on her robe, took her juice and stepped through the glass doors that opened onto the deck running the length of his room. Like hers, it over-looked the sea and pool. To the left, a crew was at work dismantling the tent and carting away the tables, chairs and assorted debris from the garden party.

She felt like calling out, take away the gossip and the speculation, too. They had no place in her life. She was a woman in love; a woman who'd been well and truly loved by her man. Her mouth was swollen from his kisses, her body tender and aching in dark and secret places. She hated the idea of washing away the scent of sex and passion that clung to her skin, and wished the day would speed to an end so that she could be alone with Dimitrios and they could make love again.

But others needed her attention first. Poor Hermione waited downstairs, alone and unsure of what her future held. Poppy waited in her hospital crib for the aunt who'd become a permanent fixture in her young and troubled life. And perhaps today Noelle would have good news about the test results and they could move to the next phase of that precious child's recovery.

In fact, for a woman who'd surely spent a sleepless night, Hermione looked remarkably serene and relaxed when Brianna finally ran her to earth in the courtyard, enjoying a breakfast of fruit and yogurt.

"I've done a lot of thinking since speaking to you at the yacht club," she said. "You're so wise, Brianna, and I owe you so much. You made me see that I have enabled Mihalis by submitting to his demands, and the sad thing is we've all lost so many years because of my weakness. I realize now that if I want to see changes, it's up to me to initiate them. And so I've begun, starting with yesterday."

"By accepting Dimitrios's invitation to come here, you mean?"

"Yes. Uniting my family is my dearest wish, but a week ago, I didn't think I had the courage to do that. Now I know differently, although I won't pretend I wasn't horrified by the scene at dinner last night. It upset me dreadfully. No woman ever wants to see her husband and son go at each other like that."

"Your husband wasn't badly hurt, Hermione," she said, helping herself to the fruit and yogurt, "Just a little shaken up."

"I know. Dimitrios explained all that. We had a long, frank talk this morning, before he left for work. Neither of us held anything back. He's not always right, you know. No one ever is. And his father isn't always wrong. At bottom, Mihalis is a very good man, but he's proud, and so is Dimitrios, and that's been the biggest obstacle to their settling their differences. My mistake has been in letting them carry on this senseless feud for so long. I should have put my foot down years ago. Well, what is it they say? Better late than never?"

The woman has more backbone than I've given her credit for, Brianna thought admiringly, *although when it comes to putting her foot down, her tiny little size sixes won't make much impression on the men in her family.*

"So," Hermione continued, "I phoned my husband a little while ago and told him I will be visiting my grand-daughter this morning."

"And how did he take it?"

"Oh, he growled and muttered, just as I knew he would, then asked when he might expect me home. I said I'd be there sometime this afternoon, and that whether or not I stayed depended on how reasonable he was prepared to be."

Brianna couldn't help herself. She hiccupped with laughter. "You did not!"

"Yes," Hermione said placidly. "I did."

"And what did he have to say to that?"

"He growled and muttered some more, but in the end asked what he should tell Artemis, our cook, to make for dinner." She laughed then, too. "I chalked that up as one victory for me."

"Do you think it's going to be that easy to change him?"

"Of course not. Nor do I really want to change him all that much. I have loved Mihalis with all his flaws for the better part of forty years. I don't relish the prospect of finding myself married to a stranger at this late date. All I want is for him to show his son and granddaughter and you the good heart he so seldom lets anyone but me ever see. Did you know, for instance, that when he heard Poppy was hospitalized, he donated a huge sum to the clinic, anonymously?"

"Dimitrios said his father refuses to acknowledge Poppy."

"Dimitrios has never brought Poppy to meet her grandfather. The last time my husband and son sat down to a meal together and exchanged anything resembling civilities was almost nine years ago. They have been estranged ever since."

"But *you* met Poppy."

"I went to see her in the hospital when she was born. Mihalis refused to come with me. He would not give Dimitrios the chance to turn him away. And Dimitrios would not give his father the chance to reject his grand-daughter."

"A vicious circle," Brianna murmured, realizing what she should have known all along: that there were always two sides to every story.

"Precisely. One that has been in effect for a very long time, and since neither of these proud, stubborn men I love so dearly will break the cycle, then I have decided that I must. And thanks to you, my dear, I feel confident that I can do so. You are the kind of woman I once was. I intend to become that woman again."

"I'm glad," Brianna said, "and, Hermione, I'm so proud of you. Hopefully, between us, we can bring about some sort of lasting peace in this family."

Hermione covered her hand. "When women stand together, they're unstoppable, so if I fall back into my old, weak ways, I shall count on you to set me straight again."

"Consider it done." She finished the last of her yogurt, drank her coffee and laid her napkin to one side. "So, what next?"

"Dimitrios thought you'd want to see Poppy."

"Yes, I spend most mornings with her. I'm usually up earlier and he drops me off at the clinic on his way to work, but I slept in today."

"That's what he said, but he didn't want to disturb you. Instead, he left instructions for Spiros to drive you to Kifissia when you're ready, and suggested I might go with you. He'll meet us for lunch later and after that…" She shrugged and made a little face. "Then I go home and face the music."

"Does that worry you, Hermione?"

"I'm a little apprehensive, I suppose. This is new territory for me, after all. But my mind is made up. From now on, Mihalis will have to dance to my tune, at least some of the time. And knowing I have you and Dimitrios behind me, well, that makes all the difference. You're very good for him, you know."

Brianna thought of the night just past and felt a blush stealing over her face. The lovemaking had been amazing and wonderful and stupendous. But there'd been so much more to it than just sex. She and Dimitrios had reached a new depth of understanding, of commitment. There'd undoubtedly be more rocky times ahead, but for the first time she really believed that together they could overcome whatever life flung at them.

"He's very good for me," she said. "We're good for each other."

Hermione nodded. "Yes. A match made in heaven."

Yesterday Brianna had questioned that. Today she almost believed it.

CHAPTER ELEVEN

SHE floated on the same cloud of optimism throughout the following week. Although no word came through on the test results, Poppy was holding her own and thrived under the extra attention of a grandmother who came to see her most days.

From all accounts, Hermione was gradually chipping away at her husband's obstreperous insistence that she choose between him and their son. "He claims my first loyalty is to my husband," she confided to Brianna on the Wednesday, her brown eyes sparkling with something close to indignation. "He says that when I married him, I promised to be a dutiful, obedient wife. I pointed out that didn't translate into my becoming his doormat."

"I shudder to think how he responded to that!"

"Actually, he was so taken aback that at first he didn't react at all. Then he glowered as only he can, and grumbled under his breath that women today were too bold and didn't know their proper place in life. And I said I knew exactly my place—it wasn't under his heel, and suggested he get used to the idea."

Was this really the same timid mouse who'd crept into the ladies' room at the yacht club less than a week ago,

Brianna wondered. But then she remembered Dimitrios telling her that his mother had once been a vivacious, spirited woman, so perhaps the person she was looking at now was the real Hermione Poulos.

"Well, I've been working on Dimitrios, too, and trying to get him to soften his attitude toward his father," she said. "He puts up a good front of pretended indifference, but I suspect he's not as averse to the idea as he pretends to be."

Hermione sighed. "I suppose, if truth be told, they're both tired of being at odds. They just don't know how to bring about an armistice without losing face."

Regardless of the issues separating Dimitrios and his father, however, between Brianna and Dimitrios blissful harmony reigned. On the Thursday night they had a picnic dinner in the quiet cove below the villa. They sat on a blanket and toasted each other with champagne. They ate salad and wonderful Greek bread Erika had baked just that morning, and big fat prawns which Dimitrios grilled over an open fire. For dessert there were fresh figs and apricots and decadent little squares of baklava. And when the fire dwindled to glowing embers and the moon rose round and yellow over the sea, he withdrew a little box from the picnic hamper and slid a dazzling two-carat diamond and platinum solitaire on her finger.

"Now it's official," he declared, lifting her hand to his mouth. "You're mine and I'll never let you go."

If he sounded a tad too triumphant, as if he'd just pulled off a business coup that left his competitors eating his dust, she supposed it was understandable. After all, they'd traveled a rough, unhappy road to get to this point, but she was finally where she'd always wanted to be, wasn't she? So why quibble over a few words uttered in the heat of the moment? Still, she couldn't help saying lightly, "This ring designates me your fiancée, Dimitrios, not a corporate acquisition."

He drew her down on the blanket and ran a possessive hand over her body. "It signifies to the whole world that you're everything I want, *chrisi mou kardia.* Everything I need."

And with the night as witness, he showed her just how deeply he wanted and needed her, making love to her with such exquisite tenderness, such masterful finesse, that her silly doubts sank into oblivion. The moon rose higher, spilling over their naked bodies in tacit blessing. The waves rolled gently ashore, whispering approval. The entire universe narrowed to a few yards of sand still warm from the day's heat, and the only man she'd ever loved.

Hermione, of course, was thrilled to see the ring on Brianna's finger. Erika clucked like a proud mother hen. Alexio and even the taciturn Spiros beamed. Just briefly the dark cloud that had hovered over the villa for so long lifted, and the sun broke through again. There was to be a wedding, a bride, a celebration.

But first, there was the gala to get through on Saturday evening. The high point of the season before people fled the summer heat of Athens and left it to the tourists, it also marked Brianna's official debut into society as the future Kyria Dimitrios Giannakis.

As usual on weekends, Dimitrios planned to spend a good part of the day with Poppy, and looked floored when Brianna said she'd go with him. "You won't have the time," he objected.

"I don't see why not," she said. "I don't have anything else to do all day."

"You mean, you haven't booked an appointment?" Then, at her uncomprehending stare, "You know—to get yourself fixed up for tonight?"

"I can fix myself up, Dimitrios," she informed him, amused. "It's one of the perks of being a model. An occupational hazard that comes with the territory, you might say. Give me an hour to get ready and I promise I won't embarrass you."

"You could never embarrass me, but you never cease to surprise me, either. Most women I know would be spending the entire day at the spa to prepare for a night on the town."

"I consider the time better spent with you and my niece. In fact, if it weren't for such a good cause, I'd be happy to miss tonight's event altogether. I don't mind admitting, after last Sunday when I felt I was under a microscope, I'm not looking forward to a repeat performance tonight."

He caught her to him and dropped a swift, hard kiss on her mouth. "Last weekend we made headlines, *agape mou.* Now we're old news and someone else has center stage."

I hope he's right, she thought later, as she checked her appearance one last time in the full-length mirror in her dressing room. She knew she looked her best. She'd pinned up her hair in a sleek chignon, and her evening gown, a lovely, narrow-skirted creation in aquamarine satin lavishly decorated with tiny crystals, was a morale booster in itself. Sleeveless, with a deep vee neck and low-cut back, it needed no enhancement beyond her engagement ring and diamond-studded platinum hoop earrings, and she shouldn't have been lacking confidence. But remembering the American women who'd been so forthcoming with their opinions at the garden party, she couldn't suppress a grimace. If she came across the one in blue again tonight, she just might pinch her.

Some four hundred people thronged the halls and gardens of one of Kifissia's grandest Victorian-style villas. A wonderful old house, with a frescoed ceiling in the ballroom, a turret at one corner and wide porches, it provided just the right touch of formal elegance to suit the occasion.

Designer gowns and priceless jewels were much in evidence, as were many of the faces Brianna had seen at the garden party. As Dimitrios had predicted, though, she was less an object of curiosity than she had been the previous weekend. She found herself relaxing and enjoying the evening as they circulated during the cocktail reception and he introduced her as his fiancée to various friends and acquaintances.

"Wonderful news," people said warmly, and "Congratulations, Dimitrios," and "Much happiness to you both."

"You see," he murmured, during a brief lull. "All your pre-gala nerves were for nothing."

Not until they found their table at dinner and she noticed an empty seat on his left did she realize Noelle hadn't shown up. "I know," Dimitrios said, when she commented. "I forgot to mention that she phoned while you were getting dressed to say she's been delayed but she'll join us later."

"Later" turned out to be almost midnight. Brianna was dancing with one of the other men from their table, leaving Dimitrios deep in conversation with two others when

Noelle arrived. All three stood up to greet her. She smiled rather wanly, shook hands, then spoke briefly to Dimitrios. He shot her a look of consternation, took her arm and quickly led her out of the ballroom.

Brianna didn't need to be clairvoyant to guess that something was amiss. "Excuse me," she muttered, and, leaving her startled dance partner performing a solo waltz, worked her way through the couples on the dance floor and hurried in the direction the other two had taken.

By then they'd disappeared and it took her several more minutes before she found them. They were not in the big entrance hall where the champagne reception had taken place, nor were they in any of the various parlors on either side.

Noticing her, a sweet-faced older woman whom she'd met earlier pointed to a closed door toward the rear of the house. "If you're looking for Dimitrios, dear," she said kindly, "I believe I saw him go into the library with Dr. Manning."

In fact, they weren't in there, either, but she heard their voices from beyond a pair of French doors opening to a covered porch, and was about to announce her presence when the gist of their conversation stopped her dead.

"Well, Dimitrios," Noelle was saying, "it's not what we hoped for, when you first suggested approaching Brianna, but I warned you then that there are never any guarantees that a parent—or in this case, a parent's identical twin— will turn out to be an acceptable donor. It's disappointing, of course…."

Disappointing? As the impact of the news struck home, Brianna recoiled as if she'd been shot in the heart. *How about* devastating, *Noelle?* She screamed silently. *How about the fact that Poppy could die because I've failed her? Will that be disappointing, too? Something we'll push to one side, in order to get on with our lives?*

Overcome with sorrow and despair, she clutched blindly at the door frame, frantic to strike some sort of bargain with God. She'd sacrifice her own health, give up Dimitrios, never again ask to be loved or to know passion and desire—anything and everything, if only Poppy could be saved.

Noelle's voice intruded again. "No point in beating yourself up, Dimitrios. You've known all along that the best possible candidate is always a sibling. But even if you and Brianna were to have a baby…"

Her words faded, lost in a burst of laughter from a group of people strolling in the garden, but it hardly mattered. The gist of what she'd been saying was clear enough, and as a second wave of shock hit, Brianna backed away from the scene, willing herself to believe she must have misunderstood.

And much, much more afraid that she finally understood all too well.

No wonder Dimitrios had been so willing to make amends, so quick to propose, so anxious to marry her as soon as possible. No wonder he *needed* her so much! Idiot that she was, she'd convinced herself he wanted her for herself. Now it all made a different kind of sense, one that had nothing to do with love—at least, not between her and him. He wanted her DNA and another child, one only she could give him.

Dear God, she might even already be pregnant!

And yet…if her having a child gave Poppy a fighting chance; was, in fact, her *only* chance…? And if, regardless of *why* she conceived, Brianna loved the baby, as she knew she would, with her whole heart, for ever and ever, would it really be so wrong…?

No. What was wrong and would always be wrong was a relationship between a man and a woman built on deception. *I don't deal well with failure,* Dimitrios had once told her. *It's not in my nature to accept defeat.*

Well, he'd certainly proved that. Even she hadn't realized the lengths he was prepared to go to, to win. He was duplicity personified. The lies and half-truths rolled off his tongue with the same facile ease as the endearments he constantly showered on her.

Sickened, she turned to leave the room. She'd heard enough and had only herself to blame if her romantic idyll had ended so abruptly and inexorably. She'd refused to listen when every instinct told her to take a step back and be sure before she once again gave everything of herself to Dimitrios.

She had wanted to believe in happily-ever-after when she'd always known that endings like that only happened in fairy tales.

If it seems too good to be true, Brianna, it usually is….

Oh, Carter, she mourned. Why didn't I pay attention to the one man in the world who's never let me down?

From the verandah, Noelle's voice again penetrated her thoughts. "…is why I'm so late. I wanted to be sure there were no last-minute hitches before I spoke to you."

Brianna couldn't bear to hear another word. Not even bothering to steal away in secret, she opened the door and let it fall shut behind her.

"So there you have it. Not the news you were hoping for, but something better. A perfect match from an unrelated donor," Noelle said. "Congratulations are definitely in order. The future's looking very bright. First you and Brianna have found each other again, and now this. She's lovely, Dimitrios, and I'm very happy for both of you." She reached up and kissed his cheek. "So, go find her and give her the excellent news."

"Come with me," he urged. "She should hear it from you."

"I'd love to, but I have a patient I need to get back to, one whose prospects are, sadly, not nearly as favorable as Poppy's."

He caught both her hands in his and squeezed them. "I owe you everything, Noelle," he said earnestly. "How do I ever repay you for all you've done?"

"By being happy for a change. Heaven knows, it's been a long time coming."

He watched her leave, then turned back into the house, eager to find Brianna. But she was not, as he expected, at their table in the ballroom, nor was she on the dance floor. She sat alone on a hard wooden bench in the grand hall, close by the front doors, her spine poker straight, her face empty of the animation she'd shown earlier, her incredible blue eyes staring sightlessly ahead.

Crossing the floor, he dropped down beside her. "Brianna, what are you doing out here?"

"Waiting for you," she replied, the chill in her voice enough to send the temperature plummeting.

Nice going, Giannakis, he thought ruefully. She knocks herself out looking gorgeous for a fancy ball she never really wanted to attend in the first place, and you leave her to fend for herself among a bunch of strangers. "Look, I'm sorry I abandoned you, sweetheart. It was unavoidable, but

I'm here now, and the night's still young. Would you like to dance?"

"No," she said flatly. "I would like to leave."

"Okay…" Baffled, he observed her more closely. He didn't particularly want to stay, either. He wanted to be alone with her, and celebrate in private news that was better than anything they could have hoped for. But he didn't have to be a rocket scientist to recognize that at this point, and for reasons he couldn't begin to fathom, she was in no mood to listen to anything he might say, let alone celebrate with him. "Brianna, what's happened? Are you not feeling well? Has someone said something to upset you?"

A brittle laugh escaped her, but her eyes, he noticed, were suddenly sheened in tears.

"Never mind," he said hastily. "Talking can wait. Let's get out of here."

Ignoring the way she shied away from him as if he had the plague, he slipped his arm around her waist and propelled her outside, and down the wide front steps to the porte-cochere where the parking valets waited. During the few minutes it took for his car to be brought round, he kept hold of her. He might as well have been hugging a marble statue.

He ushered her into the car as if she were made of china, so persuasively concerned, so convincingly tender, that it was all Brianna could do not strike out blindly and rake her nails down his beautiful, deceiving face. Instead she huddled in her seat, as far away from him as she could possibly get. Turning to the window, she stared blindly out, seeing nothing as he drove through the streets of Kifissia.

Hearing nothing but Noelle's concise summation of a situation she herself hadn't begun to guess.

…there were no guarantees…you knew from the outset the best possible candidate is always a sibling…if you and Brianna were to have a baby…

And underscoring that elegant English accent, Dimitrios's dark exotic voice and her own rash, impassioned response.

…I have no profilaktiko….

…I don't care…I want to have your baby….

Furtively she wiped at the lone tear trickling down her face. He'd hurt her before, but never like this. She felt emotionally bruised, battered and betrayed. Flayed to the bone by his deception, every loving touch, every passionate encounter, every whispered endearment exposed for the lies they were. It had all been a big sham from start to finish. He'd bamboozled her into believing he loved her, when all he really wanted was to use her.

Except, she realized with another cold sense of shock, he'd never actually used the word *love.* Never once come right out and said, "I love you." Rather, he'd told her he wanted her and he needed her. And now she knew why. Knew it had nothing to do with love and everything to do with expedience.

They'd left the lights of the city behind and were headed down the eastern slopes of Mount Penteli when he finally spoke, and this time he sounded every bit as hard and callous as she now knew him to be. "Okay, Brianna, I've had about enough of the silent treatment. I can't fix the problem if I don't know what it is, so how about spelling it out for me?"

Struggling to keep her voice steady, she said, "There is no problem. I have decided I can't marry you, that's all."

"I see. And why is that?" he inquired evenly.

"Because I don't want a husband who sees me only as a means to an end."

"What the devil are you talking about?"

Tired of the games, she said, "I followed you tonight, when you went off with Noelle. I heard her tell you I didn't measure up as a donor for Poppy."

"Is that what this is all about?" He actually had the gall to laugh. "Sweetheart, it's not a question of your not measuring up, it's—"

"A question of how soon you can get me pregnant. Yes, I heard that, too.

"What?" There was no laughter this time, just well-feigned incredulity, which she didn't buy for a second.

"'The ideal donor is always a sibling,'" she recited in her best imitation of Noelle's precise English diction.

"And?"

"And I'm the only woman still alive who can give you a child whose DNA will match Poppy's. If that's all you ever wanted from me, why didn't you just say so in the first place, and spare us both this masquerade?"

By then they'd reached the coast and were just minutes away from the villa. "Let me get this straight," he said, slowing to let a cat cross the road. "You can't donate bone marrow to Poppy, but if you have my baby, we can use it in your place, instead?"

"That's right. I should be wearing your ring through my nose, not on my finger."

He turned into the drive, parked at the front door and killed the engine, but made no move to get out of the car. Instead he hefted the keys in his palm and stared through the darkened windshield at the moonlit walls of the house.

"Whatever happened to the idea of truth and trust between us, Brianna? You're the only woman I've ever loved. Why isn't that enough for you?"

"Because your idea of love isn't the same as mine. As for truth and trust, they're just a couple of five-letter words you throw into the mix whenever you think they might get you what you want."

"I wanted you," he said harshly. "I thought we had the ideal recipe for marital bliss. Sexual electricity, desire, passion, yearning—everything we had before, except *this* time, it was better because we believed in one another. And all the time, the same vital ingredient was missing. You never could quite bring yourself to accept that what we had was real. I'm surprised you're still here. Usually you don't bother to stop long enough to say why, before you decide to cut and run."

"Don't worry. I'll be gone tomorrow."

"Thanks for the warning. I'll try to come up with an explanation for Poppy when she asks about you."

"I won't desert Poppy. I love her dearly and I'd do anything in my power to make her well. And now, if you'll excuse me, I have some packing to do. I'll let you know which hotel I'm at, in case you need to reach me."

She flung open the car door, but before she could escape, he wrenched her back and pinned her to the seat. "Oh, no, you don't!" he snarled. "This is one time you'll stay and listen."

"I don't want to hear anything you have to say."

"I don't care! First, I have a piece of advice you'd do well to heed. The next time you decide to eavesdrop on someone else's conversation, do yourself a favor and make sure you listen in on everything before you leap to unwarranted conclusions."

"Thank you so much," she said acidly. "Anything else you feel compelled to share?"

"Yes," he replied. "I am not Poppy's biological father."

It was her turn to stare in disbelief. "What did you say?"

"I am not Poppy's biological father, I have no idea who is, and nor do I care. She is my daughter in every way that matters, and I would give my life for her. *That,* Brianna, is how I define love."

"But Noelle said—"

"That even if you and I were to have a child solely for the purpose of harvesting his or her stem cells, it wouldn't necessarily help Poppy and that, of course, is something I've known since the day I tested as a possible donor myself, and discovered not only that I wasn't a match but also that there was no way I could possibly be her biological parent. So you see, my dear, my proposal to you was never contingent on your acting as a brood mare. Oh, yes, and one last thing—I learned tonight that we've found an unrelated donor who's a perfect match for Poppy. That was the other piece of news Noelle wanted to convey. She'd have told both of us yesterday, when she also learned of your unsuitability. But rather than risk a second disappointment, she waited until she received absolute confirmation that the other person, a twenty-three-year-old medical student from Chile, is available. Apparently, he is and will be here on Tuesday."

He released her then and flung himself back in his seat. "You may leave now. Don't let me keep you from your packing."

CHAPTER TWELVE

THE house was silent as a tomb. Creeping up the stairs, Brianna let herself into her room and slumped onto the love seat. She wished she could cry. But she had nothing left inside. No tears, no hope and no heart. She and Dimitrios were finally over. Done. She'd heard the absolute contempt in his voice. Seen it in his face. Felt it in his touch.

Slowly, she pulled off his ring and placed it on the coffee table. She couldn't blame Cecily for this latest falling out. This time it was all her own fault. She'd been the one who lacked faith, and if she was as honest with herself as she'd told him he should have been with her, she'd admit she'd been second-guessing herself and him from the day she arrived. Now the only thing left for her to do was leave with dignity.

Or was it? Was anything ever really over as long as a person had life and the will to fight?

You're the only woman I've ever loved, he'd said, not in a moment of passion, but with anger fueling his words. Wasn't that reason enough not to give up on the best thing that had ever happened to her?

She had no answers, and knew only that if she wanted to find any, she had to put some distance between him and her. As long as his room was just across the hall from hers, it would be too easy to go to him. She knew what the outcome would be if she did: the same as it had always been with them. A matter of body over mind, of the driving hunger of the flesh silencing the saner voice of reason.

And they had made enough mistakes. There were only so many times that a man and a woman could keep trying to mend what was broken between them before all they had left were the tattered remains of what had once been beautiful but was now ruined past recognition.

Kicking off her satin dancing shoes, she stripped away her pretty gown and changed into a light cotton shift and sandals.

Opening her door, she saw a strip of light showing under his. Otherwise, the house lay in darkness. Quietly she stole along the upper landing, down the stairs and out into the sweet night air of early June. When she reached the gates, she turned left, away from Rafina, which lay to the north, and toward the village a few kilometers in the opposite direction.

Dimitrios ripped off his bow tie and yanked the top two studs of his dress shirt undone. Still he felt choked—on anger, on regret, on pride. Why couldn't she simply have come to him and asked him to explain, instead of automatically believing the worst of him? He thought they'd moved beyond that. Instead it seemed nothing he did would ever really redeem him in her eyes. At the first hint of trouble, he became again the man she believed had betrayed her before.

Well, to hell with her! He was tired of proving himself worthy of her love. Let her run back to her precious career.

He'd lived without her once before; he could do so again. He had his daughter, his loyal household staff, perhaps his mother. And if he needed a willing body once in a while, there were women enough who'd be glad to warm his bed.

But would they be enough to make him forget her, or would it always be *her* face he saw in his mind's eye, *her* body he thought of as he lost himself in some stranger whose name he'd have forgotten by morning? How long before the day came that he didn't think of her, or miss her with an ache that never went away?

Never. She was in his blood, a fatal, magnificent disease. And the cure he'd spend the rest of his life seeking, if he let her slip through his fingers a second time.

He couldn't let it happen. If he had to get down on his knees and plead with her to stay, he'd do it, and pride be damned.

Stepping out of his room, he saw a strip of light showing under her door. No time like the present, he decided. Tomorrow might be too late. Crossing the hall, he tapped gently, and when he received no reply, he turned the knob and went in.

He knew then why she hadn't answered. The room was empty.

Although it was well after midnight, the village teemed with life. Music and light spilled from open windows into the warm Mediterranean night. Children played in the street, dogs barked, babies cried. Men and women, husbands and wives, laughed and loved and scolded, daring to wring every last drop of flavor from life because it was worth it and in the end, the good balanced out the bad.

The four-kilometer walk had cleared Brianna's mind and swept away the anger and confusion. Standing now, a solitary spectator on the fringe of the scene, she knew that *this* was what she wanted. Not perfection. Not a trouble-free future with no dark clouds. She wanted the security of knowing she could be angry sometimes; of loving deeply enough to forgive; of trusting enough to believe what she and Dimitrios shared was strong enough to survive, not because they'd ironed out all their differences, but despite the fact that they didn't always see eye to eye.

She wanted all the rich flavors, all the subtle textures that made up a marriage. The sweet and the not-so-sweet. The rough and the smooth. She wanted him because without him, she was nothing. She needed him because she loved him. And there in that dusty road, surrounded by strangers, she at last realized what she had to do to keep him. She had to risk it all to have him.

She'd turned to go back the way she'd come, when the screech of brakes split the night. Parents scooped their children out of the path of impending danger and retreated to the safety of their doorways. But the speeding car had stopped at the far end of the road and a tall, familiar figure was climbing out.

A wonderful lightness filled her then, and slowly she started toward him. Then suddenly she was running and so was he, and they met in a breathless meshing of arms and mouths, and she was crying helplessly, and he was telling her he was sorry, that it was all his fault and he should have explained about Poppy sooner and he was nothing but a big, arrogant Greek fool with too much pride and not enough brains, and if she ever took off like that again without telling him where she was going, he'd put her over his knee.

Eventually the tumult passed and they drew apart. He took a deep breath and so did she. "Let's go home," he said, surely the sweetest words in the world.

"Yes," she said. "Please."

The next second he was carrying her to the car, while everyone in the village clapped and whistled, and the bouzouki music started up again, loud and exuberant.

"I thought I'd lost you," he whispered, holding her so tight she could hardly breathe. "When I saw you'd gone…Brianna, I once told you I don't beg, but I'm begging now. Don't leave me. Don't give up on us."

She wrapped her arms around his neck. "I won't," she told him, smiling through her tears. "Never again. I was coming back to tell you so, but then you were here and…"

"And I'm never letting you out of my sight again. If you want Poppy, you have to take me, as well. We're a package deal."

"And a bargain at half the price. I know that now."

They sat on the love seat in her room, and the first thing he did was slide the ring back on her finger. "Just to let the rest of the world know you're taken," he said, settling back with his arm around her.

After that, they talked far into the small hours of the night, hours longer than they'd ever done before. About how, after they'd made love by the pool after the garden party, he'd almost told her about Poppy not being his biological child, and how later, he was glad he'd kept quiet because he'd tarnished Cecily's memory enough and he wanted to leave Brianna with some of her illusions intact.

About Poppy and what she faced in the coming months. About finally closing the door on the past. About how much they'd both always craved marriage and children and family. And most important of all, about priorities.

"I agree," he admitted, when she said the wedding should be put on hold. "As long as we're together, it can wait until everything else is sorted out. Assuming the transplant does go ahead without any complications, Poppy's facing a lengthy recuperation."

"There's also the small matter of you and your father getting past your differences and reaching some sort of truce. This ridiculous feud has gone on long enough, and you have to know how hard it is on your mother. Even though you and she have reconciled, she's still caught in the middle. Put an end to it, Dimitrios, for everyone's sake. You made your point. He got the message. Can't you please leave it at that and just sit down with him, man to man, and try to heal the wounds?"

"Hmm." He eyed her gloomily. "Are you going to make a habit of always being right?"

"Only when it can't be avoided," she said, snuggling deeper into the curve of his arm. "Which'll probably be most of the time."

She felt the laughter rumble deep in his chest. "Is there anything else I should know?"

"Just that I love you, I always have, and that will never change."

"That's all I ask," he murmured against her hair, and took her to bed to seal their bargain.

The passion consumed them, as it always had, but in its wake came a new serenity, a sense of absolute certainty that while trouble and sorrow might touch their tomorrow, their love would do more than survive. It would emerge triumphant.

She was where she belonged. At his side.

EPILOGUE

A COLD February rain dripped from the palm trees, but inside the villa walls, fires chased away the chill of the winter afternoon, and the scent of gardenias filled the rooms with summer.

In her bedroom Brianna fixed the coronet of rosebuds more securely in Poppy's hair, which had grown back thicker and more lustrous than ever after her chemotherapy. "You look adorable, my angel."

Poppy twirled before the mirror, sending the skirt of her pale-pink flower girl's dress flaring around her ankles. "I'm not an angel, I'm a princess."

Brianna exchanged a smiling glance with Hermione. "She's a miracle."

"One of many lately," Hermione replied fondly, "and I give thanks for them every day. You've done more than fill my son's life with love and happiness, Brianna. You've given me back my family. I never thought to see the day that Mihalis would stand up as best man for Dimitrios at his wedding." She dabbed at her eyes and gave a little laugh. "Dear me, I promised myself I wouldn't cry today, and look at me. I'm not even waiting for the ceremony to begin before I get started."

"Don't," Brianna begged. "You'll get me going, too, and we've shed enough tears in the past eight months to last us a lifetime."

Even on this, the happiest day of her life so far, the specter of those dark days after the transplant still haunted her. She still sometimes woke up in the middle of the night, terrified and soaked in sweat, tears streaming down her face, caught again in the nightmare of agony of watching Poppy suffer the nausea, the fever, the pain and debilitating weakness that were part and parcel of the cure.

She'd never forget the suspense of waiting for signs that the new bone marrow had migrated and was beginning to produce normal blood cells. For weeks on end, every time the phone rang, she and Dimitrios would freeze, fearing the worst.

The emotional highs and lows, the unending stress, had almost killed them. Yet it had made them stronger, too. "If we can survive this," he'd often said, "we can survive anything."

But whoever first said God never closed a door without first opening a window, had it right. One day she'd looked up from her post with Dimitrios beside Poppy's hospital crib, and seen Mihalis standing with Hermione on the other side of the observation window, his chin quivering and tears rolling down his face. Dimitrios had been a rock until then, but at that, he'd buried his face in his hands and his whole body had shaken with great, heaving sobs.

Heavens, yes. They'd all cried enough tears to fill a lake. They didn't need more today.

Fortunately, Carter knocked on the door just then, timing his arrival to prevent a complete emotional meltdown. "You're running late, ladies, and the groom's growing impatient."

"We're ready," Hermione said, letting him in. "Come along, Poppy, my darling. We'll go ahead and give Mommy Brianna a moment to collect herself."

Alone with Carter, Brianna managed a smile. "Thank you for being here, Carter."

"Try keeping me away! You're a picture, you know that? And I'm a damn fool to be giving away the best client I ever had. I hope that Greek god you're so crazy about realizes how lucky he is."

"We're both lucky," she said tremulously. "And you're a lot more than just my former agent, Carter. You've been my best friend for more years than I care to count, and I don't know how I'll ever repay you for all you've done for me."

"I do," he said, kissing her cheek. "Be happy. That's payment enough for me."

"You've got the rings?"

"Right here." His father patted his pocket, then cleared his throat and stepped closer. "Just wanted to say…well, I'm here and you're here and…well, that young woman upstairs, she's all right. You're both all right, and I'm…well, I'm here. If you need me. Which you probably don't."

"I need you, Dad," he said. "I always have."

"Huh. Well, it took some doing. You're a stubborn cuss when you put your mind to it, just like me, but— Stop sweating. You're making me nervous."

Dimitrios buried a grin.

A murmur from the sixty friends and associates filling

the hall had him looking up. His mother was coming down the stairs, holding his daughter by the hand, and suddenly he was so choked with emotion he could hardly swallow. The pale, listless little waif he'd worried about and fretted over for so long had turned into a sweetly rounded sprite whose cheeks were as pink as the rosebuds in her hair.

"Cut it out," his father muttered brokenly. "The men in this family don't cry in public."

Behind him, all the people who'd helped him come to this day—Erika and Alexio, Noelle and everyone else who'd given his daughter back her life, friends he hadn't known he had until he needed them and they were there for him—every last one rose from their ribbon-festooned chairs as the harpist tucked in the lee of the curving staircase segued from Debussy's "Claire de Lune," to Wagner's "Bridal Chorus."

And suddenly, there she was, his bride, his Brianna, descending the stairs with the innate grace she brought to everything she did, her hand resting lightly on Carter's arm, her ivory silk gown billowing around her, her lovely face shadowed by a gossamer veil.

He'd been wrong to think she'd lose her looks with age. Wrong to believe she'd have nothing left. Hers was a beauty carved from love, from compassion and deep generosity of spirit. It would cloak her features with softness, illuminate her from within, when she was old and gray and youth was but a memory. She would always be a beauty. His beauty, his life.

She was closer now, covering the last few meters that separated her from him, carving a graceful path through the rose petals Poppy was flinging enthusiastically before her.

He squared his shoulders and held out his hand. Her

fingers closed around his, warm and firm and sure. His father was crying; his mother, too. But Brianna was radiant, her smile for him alone.

He was home at last.

Harlequin Presents brings you
a brand-new duet by star author

Sharon Kendrick

Power, pride and passion—discover how only
the love and passion of two women can reunite
these wealthy, successful brothers,
divided by a bitter rivalry.

Available June 2008:

THE GREEK TYCOON'S
BABY BARGAIN

Available July 2008:

THE GREEK TYCOON'S
CONVENIENT WIFE

EXTRA

TALL, DARK AND SEXY
The men who never fail—seduction included!

Brooding, successful and arrogant, these men
can sweep any female they desire off her feet.
But now there's only one woman they want—
and they'll use their wealth, power, charm and
irresistibly seductive ways to claim her!

**Don't miss any of the titles in this exciting
collection available June 10, 2008:**

#9 THE BILLIONAIRE'S VIRGIN BRIDE
by HELEN BROOKS

#10 HIS MISTRESS BY MARRIAGE
by LEE WILKINSON

#11 THE BRITISH BILLIONAIRE AFFAIR
by SUSANNE JAMES

#12 THE MILLIONAIRE'S MARRIAGE REVENGE
by AMANDA BROWNING

*Harlequin Presents EXTRA delivers a themed
collection every month featuring 4 new titles.*

I ♥ HARLEQUIN® *Presents*

BROUGHT TO YOU BY FANS OF
HARLEQUIN PRESENTS.

We are its editors and authors
and biggest fans—and we'd
love to hear from YOU!

Subscribe today to our online blog at
www.iheartpresents.com

REQUEST YOUR FREE BOOKS!

HARLEQUIN *Presents*

2 FREE NOVELS PLUS 2
FREE GIFTS!

PASSION GUARANTEED SEDUCTION

YES! Please send me 2 FREE Harlequin Presents® novels and my 2 FREE gifts (gifts are worth about $10). After receiving them, if I don't wish to receive any more books, I can return the shipping statement marked "cancel". If I don't cancel, I will receive 6 brand-new novels every month and be billed just $4.05 per book in the U.S. or $4.74 per book in Canada, plus 25¢ shipping and handling per book and applicable taxes, if any*. That's a savings of close to 15% off the cover price! I understand that accepting the 2 free books and gifts places me under no obligation to buy anything. I can always return a shipment and cancel at any time. Even if I never buy another book, the two free books and gifts are mine to keep forever.   106 HDN ERRW 306 HDN ERRL

Name _____ (PLEASE PRINT) _____

Address _____ Apt. # _____

City _____ State/Prov. _____ Zip/Postal Code _____

Signature (if under 18, a parent or guardian must sign)

Mail to the **Harlequin Reader Service:**
IN U.S.A.: P.O. Box 1867, Buffalo, NY 14240-1867
IN CANADA: P.O. Box 609, Fort Erie, Ontario L2A 5X3

Not valid to current subscribers of Harlequin Presents books.

Want to try two free books from another line?
Call 1-800-873-8635 or visit www.morefreebooks.com.

* Terms and prices subject to change without notice. N.Y. residents add applicable sales tax. Canadian residents will be charged applicable provincial taxes and GST. Offer not valid in Quebec. This offer is limited to one order per household. All orders subject to approval. Credit or debit balances in a customer's account(s) may be offset by any other outstanding balance owed by or to the customer. Please allow 4 to 6 weeks for delivery. Offer available while quantities last.

Your Privacy: Harlequin Books is committed to protecting your privacy. Our Privacy Policy is available online at www.eHarlequin.com or upon request from the Reader Service. From time to time we make our lists of customers available to reputable third parties who may have a product or service of interest to you. If you would prefer we not share your name and address, please check here. ☐

HP08R

EXTRA

THE BOSS'S MISTRESS

Out of the office…and into his bed

These ruthless, powerful men are used
to having their own way in the office—
and with their mistresses they're also
boss in the bedroom!

**Don't miss any of our fantastic stories
in the July 2008 collection:**

www.eHarlequin.com

HPE0708